RUN, RUN, AS FAST AS YOU CAN

BOOKS BY WILLOW ROSE

Emma Frost Mysteries
Itsy Bitsy Spider
Miss Polly Had a Dolly
Cross Your Heart and Hope to Die
Peek a Boo, I See You
Tweedledum and Tweedledee
Easy as One, Two, Three
There's No Place Like Home
Needles and Pins
Where the Wild Roses Grow
Waltzing Matilda
Drip Drop Dead
Black Frost

Detective Billie Ann Wilde series
Don't Let Her Go
Then She's Gone
In Her Grave

RUN, RUN, AS FAST AS YOU CAN

WILLOW ROSE

bookouture

Published by Bookouture in 2024

An imprint of Storyfire Ltd.
Carmelite House
50 Victoria Embankment
London EC4Y 0DZ

www.bookouture.com

Copyright © Willow Rose, 2024

Willow Rose has asserted her right to be identified
as the author of this work.

First published by Buoy Media LLC in 2013.

All rights reserved. No part of this publication may be reproduced, stored in any retrieval system, or transmitted, in any form or by any means, electronic, mechanical, photocopying, recording or otherwise, without the prior written permission of the publishers.

ISBN: 978-1-83525-325-0
eBook ISBN: 978-1-83525-324-3

This book is a work of fiction. Names, characters, businesses, organisations, places and events other than those clearly in the public domain, are either the product of the author's imagination or are used fictitiously. Any resemblance to actual persons, living or dead, events or locales is entirely coincidental.

CONTENT NOTE

This book features graphic scenes of violence. If this is potentially sensitive to you, please read with care.

PROLOGUE

She felt like someone was watching her. Simone Beaumont turned her head and looked around the parking lot behind the shop selling children's clothes, where she had just found a new winter jacket for her oldest son. In her arms, she was holding Liv, her nine-month-old baby.

Simone didn't like the feeling of being watched, but the parking lot was empty except for one other car parked far away from hers. It was late in the afternoon, and the sun had gone down an hour ago. Simone grunted and looked up at the dark sky above her. How she loathed these Danish winters with all the darkness. Simone loved the sun, but as soon as they reached the end of September, it got darker really fast and there was a long time of darkness ahead of them. That was the worst part about November. It was always so gray and dark and rainy. Last year it rained for twenty-five days in a row in November. Simone really hoped that wouldn't be the case this year.

"Come on, sweetie, let's go home," she said to Liv, whom she held in her arms, as she opened the door to her car. Liv was grumpy and complained when Simone put her in her car seat.

She never did like the stupid seat, and Simone had a struggle every time.

"No. No, Liv. You need to be strapped down," she said to her daughter with a firm voice. Simone's neck hurt and she put a hand on it to massage it. It had been like this for months now. Maybe she should see a doctor about it after all.

Finally she managed to hold her daughter still long enough to strap her down properly. Simone moaned in pain and moved her head slowly. She knew perfectly well why she hadn't gone to see her doctor about this yet. She was so afraid that he was going to tell her it was a whiplash injury.

Simone had been certain the neck problems would disappear on their own, but eight months after the accident, they still hadn't.

"There we go, Liv," she said to her whining daughter, who clearly wasn't happy about having to sit in the seat. "Now let's go home."

Simone closed the door to the car. She paused before opening her own door and looked at her daughter through the window. Liv's mouth was wide open and, through the glass, she could hear her crying.

Just going to be one of those things you have to ignore.

Why was it that nothing about having children was easy? Why hadn't anyone told her up front how hard it was going to be?

Nobody tells you about the constant crying and the pressure and stress. No one. Simone had to learn on her own. In the beginning, she thought there was something terribly wrong with Liv because she cried so much, and Anthony never cried like that when he was a baby. But then, she met other women in her mothers' group, and they told her that it wasn't Liv who had something wrong, it was Anthony who had just been a very quiet child. Their little babies cried too and drove them nuts every now and then.

Simone sighed and stared at her crying daughter. She really didn't want to have to listen to that all the way home. Thank God for her mothers' group. Without them she would have run away a long time ago. She liked all four of the other women in that group, even Lisa. Even if she did tend to be a little too perfectionistic every now and then and brag about how healthy she was and how she couldn't understand how anyone could feed their kids gluten. She did make some nice smoothies though, and she often brought some for the group to taste. They were really good.

Simone felt eyes on her again and turned to look one last time.

It's just your mind playing tricks on you, Simone. Like yesterday when you felt like someone was looking at you through your living room window. Let it go before you get all paranoid.

Simone chuckled and shook her head. Her husband Tim had been laughing at her for the past week, telling her how paranoid she was and asking where it suddenly came from.

"I don't know. It's just this feeling," she had tried to explain to him, but she knew by the look in his eyes that he didn't understand. He didn't want to understand. Ever since they had Liv, he thought of her as some over-compulsive, obsessive, neurotic woman who was constantly on the verge of losing her mind completely. It was true that her behavior had been quite irrational, especially after an incident earlier this year where she thought she had lost Liv. Yes, it had left her feeling a little overly protective of the girl, but so what? Wasn't that only natural after almost losing your daughter?

Simone shook her head once again and felt the excruciating pain in her neck. She drew in a deep breath considering, just for a short second, just running away from everything. She really didn't want to sit in the car listening to her baby scream all the way home, nor did she want to go back to the house and face Tim. Their fight last night hadn't made things better. She was still angry with him and hadn't spoken to him all morning. But it wasn't just the fight that made her reconsider her future with him. It was more the way he constantly made her feel like she was all wrong.

Simone reached out to grab the door handle when she heard a sound coming from behind her. With a small gasp, she turned around, not thinking about the pain in her neck anymore, and looked directly into the eyes of a man. He was smiling in a daunting manner.

"You're the one who's been watching me, aren't you?" she asked, surprised by her own courage.

The man didn't answer. Instead he reached out his hand and grabbed her, covering her mouth and nose with a strong-smelling cloth. The last thing Simone heard before she blacked out was the sound of her daughter crying helplessly inside the car.

ONE

OCTOBER 2003

Thomas was whistling while putting on his jacket. He glanced at himself in the mirror and corrected his hair one last time, then picked up the bouquet of flowers. He smiled and held them high, pretending to give them to her.

"These are for you, Ellen," he said.

No, no. Don't smile like that. It makes you look creepy. You're supposed to be nice, remember?

Thomas exhaled and looked at his own reflection. Was he kidding himself? He was so ugly it almost hurt, and she was so beautiful, he had no words for it. Yet, she had still chosen him, hadn't she? He was the lucky guy who she had set her sights on; he was the one she wanted. He knew he was. He had seen it in her eyes when she looked at him and smiled. And things had been well between them ever since that day she walked out of the bank and they bumped into each other accidentally. She had dropped the papers in her hand and he had helped her pick them up afterward. Then, she smiled at him and their eyes locked. Ever since that day, Thomas's life had been turned upside down. Nothing was ever the same again. He couldn't sleep, he couldn't work, and he could hardly eat anything. All he did was think of her and her spectacular blonde hair. Thomas couldn't remember ever feeling like this before and had started wondering if this was it. Could this be the real deal? Could this be true love?

The thought made Thomas blush and smile again. He glanced in the mirror and saw his own reflection. Once again he was struck by his own hideousness and the feeling of despair hit him like so many times before.

How could she ever love a buffoon like you?

Thomas exhaled deeply again, then turned away from the mirror and started walking outside. It didn't matter how he felt about himself. As long as she was in his life, nothing could bring him down; he wasn't going to listen to those voices inside of him telling him he was no good, that he would never be loved.

"Everybody deserves to be loved," he mumbled as he walked outside through the rain toward his car.

He put the flowers on the passenger seat and drove off toward her house in the town of Nordby on Fanoe island. The wipers were whispering in the rain. It was like the sky was crying, but it didn't matter to Thomas. Today he wasn't going to be depressed or discouraged by anything. He was going to see his loved one and nothing was going to ruin his perfect mood. He was happy for once in his life.

Thomas parked the car on her street, then looked out the window through the raindrops. The curtains in all the windows were shut. Thomas smiled. That was her secret signal for him. Only the two of them knew what it meant. Thomas felt butterflies in his stomach. Being close to her always did that to him. He had a great night planned for the two of them. He had reserved a table at La Petite Cuisine downtown, even if it was a little too expensive for him; then they would take a stroll down to the port and watch the ferry come in. It looked so beautiful at night with all its lights. Thomas had always loved the port. His own dad used to take him down there on Sundays to buy an ice cream and watch the ferry come in from the mainland. Thomas still remembered looking at all the cars as they drove off the ferry and all the happy people walking from the deck onto the quay. His dad would tell him that the island lived off of these tourists and he should be very happy that they came and brought all their money with them. The port and the ferry had been a big part of Thomas's life and still were. His dad had worked as a port engineer and so did Thomas. He wanted Ellen to know and to see the beauty of the ferry like he did. He knew she would understand why this place was so important. She would see it because he did. She would love it because he did.

Thomas drew in a deep breath, then opened the door to the car and stepped outside in the pouring rain, holding the flowers in his hand. He ran toward Ellen's house, but then something happened that made him stop. The door opened and Ellen came out, but she wasn't alone. She was with somebody and seeing them together made everything stop inside of Thomas. The person stepping outside the door with her was a man. A tall and very handsome man. He smiled widely, then leaned over and kissed her passionately on the lips. Thomas felt like his heart had stopped.

TWO
NOVEMBER 2013

"I'm home."

I rolled my suitcase into the living room and spotted Maya sitting next to my dad, reading a book. Victor was sitting on the floor writing numbers in his notebook, something he had done a lot lately.

"Hello? Is anyone home? I'm back," I said.

My dad lifted his head and smiled. Maya did the same. "Hi, Mom," she said.

"How was your trip?" my dad asked.

"Great," I said and threw my jacket on the back of the chair. "Don't I get a welcome home hug?"

Maya rolled her eyes, then got up and gave me a reluctant hug. I took it and held her tight. I had missed her like crazy and, even if it was a reluctant hug, I was taking what I could get. Especially because I wasn't going to get one from Victor.

"Mmm, I missed you," I said, as she tore herself free from my arms. She rolled her eyes at me again.

"Mom, you were only gone for a week."

My dad gave me a kiss on the cheek. "So, did you find any of the lost children?" he asked as we sat down. It felt so good to be back home again. A week in Poland made me appreciate my own home a little more, especially the parts of Poland I had been through.

I shook my head. "No. We got a little closer though. We tracked one of the girls, Tenna, who disappeared in 1998 to a small brothel in a small town named Poznań. But the trail ended there, unfortunately. No one remembered her or knew what had happened to her since then. So, I guess we're back where we started."

My dad exhaled and leaned back on the couch. Maya put her head on his shoulder. The two of them had gotten really close lately and it pleased me immensely, even if I was a little jealous. It was good for her to have a male role model, now that her dad had pulled out of her life completely.

"It's like finding a needle in a haystack, huh?" he said.

"It is. But I have a feeling that it will happen one day. I mean these girls can't just have disappeared, can they?"

"Well... yes, as a matter of fact, they can," my dad said. "Not to try to destroy your hope, but they could have been killed and buried in the ground without anyone blinking. They were stolen and sold as slaves to people who did what they pleased with them. People who have no respect for human lives. Did you at least get some stuff for your next book?"

I nodded. "I have so much material, it's overwhelming. Did you see that *Miss Polly Had a Dolly* hit the bestseller list this week?"

My dad nodded. "Yes and I'm very proud of you. I can't believe you now have two national bestsellers."

I chuckled. "Me either." I looked at my dad. I was happy to see him so calm, even if he was still suffering from his broken heart.

"Talked to your mom lately?" he asked.

"I called her from Poland. She invited us to Spain, but, as usual, I refused. Told her we don't have time."

"You should go, Emma. Don't punish your mother for the rest of her life. You'll regret it when she's gone."

"Do you regret not having spent more time with your mother after all she did to you?" I asked.

My dad shrugged. "I guess not. But still. She is your only mother."

"I hate her for leaving you," I said.

My dad sighed. "Hate is such a strong word. I'm angry with her too, but I still think you need her in your life."

"That might be true, but I'm too busy now to go visit her. Besides, the kids have their school and, with the new book, I want to write about the parents searching for their lost children; I really can't see when I will be able to go."

"I have to say, I'm really looking forward to this one," he said.

"You should see them, Dad. That look in their eyes, the small hope that they might find their daughter again. It's so heartbreaking, especially when the search doesn't lead to anything. But they have been so grateful. Tenna's parents, whom we followed on this trip, were just so thankful that we had found out more about where their daughter had been. I just wish we had found her."

"And how was traveling with Officer Bredballe?" Maya asked teasingly.

"Morten has been so great through everything. He's the one doing all the work, really. I only tag along and interview the parents along the way. He's the one tracking the girls down, through police channels and helpers in the Polish underground. It's like a puzzle, but he has been amazing."

"I bet he has," Maya said.

I ignored her remark. Yes I had been traveling a lot with Morten these last months on these trips and, yes, we had had several dinners and talked for hours in the hotel lobbies, but that was all.

I got up from my chair, then walked over and kneeled next to Victor. "Hi, buddy. Mommy's back. How have you been?"

Victor didn't even look at me. I wondered if he had even noticed that I had been gone. He kept writing numbers in his notebook like it was the most important thing in the entire world. I sighed and rose to my feet again. "So what does a girl have to do to get a cup of coffee around here?"

THREE
NOVEMBER 2013

Lisa Rasmussen was running as fast as she could on the treadmill at the local fitness center in Nordby. In the body-sized mirrors covering the walls, she could see her butt that still seemed three sizes bigger than before she had her third child.

She had moved to Fanoe island less than a year ago and was still adjusting to the island lifestyle here. She did enjoy the wide sandy beaches and the fresh cold air blowing from the north, making her feel refreshed and strong again. But everything seemed so small here and people were just so... so incredibly slow. It annoyed her to have to wait for her lunch at Café Mimosa, the only one serving organic, low-carb and fat-reduced, non-gluten food on the entire island. It annoyed her that there was only one supermarket in the entire town and that it didn't sell her favorite brand of tofu.

Lisa sighed as she stopped running. She showered and gathered her things, then drove home. Her nine-month-old baby was whining in the backseat and Lisa tried to calm her down by singing her favorite song.

Rock-a-bye baby, on the treetop,

*When the wind blows, the cradle will rock,
When the bough breaks, the cradle will fall,
And down will come baby, cradle and all.*

Margrethe seemed to calm down a little once she heard her mother's gentle voice. It pleased Lisa. She parked the car in the garage, then took Margrethe out of her car seat. She started whimpering again, then she gripped Lisa's hair and pulled it. It hurt, but Lisa kept calm.

Once inside, she put Margrethe in the playpen, then started making dinner. One after another, Amalie and Jacob came home and she fed them sandwiches before she told them to go upstairs and do their homework.

Christian came home a little past six o'clock and wanted a beer before dinner, but Lisa told him he couldn't have it.

"It'll ruin your appetite."

Grumbling he went to the living room and turned on the TV. The new job was going well for him. That was why they chose to move here, because of a job offer he couldn't resist. Lisa was pleased to be able to support his career. She used to have one too, but since they had Amalie eleven years ago, she had stopped working at her career, wanting to be there for her family. It was very unusual in Denmark, where most women seemed to want big careers.

Lisa peeled the potatoes while shaking her head, thinking about her stroll in the park earlier in the day. All that rubbish that people threw everywhere. It was disgusting. And why wasn't anyone cleaning it up? This was a nice town and should remain that way.

Lisa kept peeling a potato and didn't realize she had cut herself. She gasped as she saw the blood run from her index finger into the sink, dripping onto the potatoes. She looked at the blood running down her finger for quite a while, studying closely how it found its way down and how the drops were shaped at the end. Why some women didn't like to see blood, she couldn't understand. To Lisa there was something so fascinating about it, so alluring that she couldn't stop staring at it.

"When will dinner be ready?" Christian asked, as he stepped inside the kitchen.

Quickly, Lisa turned on the tap and washed the finger. Then she found a paper towel and wrapped the finger in it before she turned to face him.

"Sorry, honey. What was that?"

"I asked when dinner would be ready. I'm starving."

"I'm working on it," she said.

"Could you give me an estimate? Is it like half an hour or an hour? 'Cause then I'll probably go down to the bar and meet with the guys from work."

"I guess it's more like half an hour," she lied, knowing he wouldn't have enough time to go.

"So, is it precisely half an hour or more like half an hour? 'Cause I could easily make it down and back real fast if I left now."

Lisa took the potato peeler in her hand and imagined stabbing Christian with it in his throat. She pictured how he would look at her, startled, taken aback, searching for an answer, while she would just look at the blood running down his torso, wondering if she would ever be able to get it all off his white shirt.

"Lisa?" he said.

Lisa looked at him with a distant smile. "I'm serving salmon for dinner," she said, then turned around and grabbed another potato in her hand.

FOUR
NOVEMBER 2013

It was completely dark when she opened her eyes. Simone felt dizzy and tried to sit up, but had to put her head back on the floor to not lose consciousness again. It took a few minutes before she remembered.

"Liv," she mumbled and tried to lift her head again. Pictures of her crying daughter on the back seat of the car flickered in front of her eyes. "Where is Liv?" she said a little louder. "Tim?" she called out.

But there was no answer.

"Where am I?" she asked the darkness.

Desperately, she tried to feel the floor around her. Something crackled when she touched it. She stretched out to try to reach farther away. It seemed the floor was all covered in what felt like newspapers. Simone tried to crawl across it while feeling her way with her fingers. Her hand bumped into something. It was an edge of some sort. It felt like wood. She touched it and felt it upward. The wood stopped but now there was something else blocking her way. Something that made her heart stop. It was wire. She felt it again. It had holes that she could put her fingers through. Was it a net? Or maybe some kind of wired fence?

Simone tried to feel how far it went, but the darkness scared her. She was afraid of moving too much and falling and hurting herself. Why was it so dark? There had to be some kind of light somewhere. She turned her head to try to find any kind of light, something coming from a window or under a door. There seemed to be a little light coming from somewhere far away from her, near the floor. Probably a door, she thought. Maybe it was a way out. At least there had to be a light switch near the door, right?

The newspapers crackled underneath her as she moved frantically around, feeling her way toward the light, but she was stopped by more wire fence. She was sobbing slightly now, wondering where she was and how she had gotten there, but most of all fearing that something had happened to her daughter.

Oh, God, please let me see her again. Please don't let anything happen to her. I promise I'll never complain about her crying again. I promise I'll never dream about running away. I didn't mean it, God. I really didn't. I was just tired and exhausted. You know that, don't you?

The thought that something might have happened to her daughter fed the growing panic. Where was she? Was she still in the car? Was she still crying in the back seat? Who would find her there?

"Tim?" she called again. "Hello? Is there anyone who can hear me?"

She grabbed the fence and tried to pull herself up to her feet. She succeeded, despite the strong dizziness, only to realize she couldn't stand up straight. Her head hit some sort of ceiling made from more wire. Simone gasped and patted it to feel how big it was. That was when her hand accidentally touched something that made her pull back and throw herself back to the floor with a whimper. She curled up in the corner and looked up to see if she could spot what it was that she had touched. It had felt soft and warm. There was no doubt in Simone's mind that it had been an animal of some kind. Simone shivered and stared into the darkness. She sensed movement. There was a sound. Yes, something was definitely up there. She wasn't alone.

What is this place? Where am I? Please someone get me out of here. Oh, Tim, please find me.

Simone heard more movement from above her and looked up with a gasp. Something touched the net and made a loud noise, like it was grabbing on to it. Simone stared into the darkness and wondered. Those small dots that were constantly moving. Were those eyes looking at her?

Another sound startled her. A small shriek almost like a bird or a baby crying. But it wasn't a bird or a baby, that much she knew. The sound was too different, much different from anything she had ever heard before. Sometimes it was like screaming, then more like a clicking.

Then something came toward her. She saw it move and sensed it come closer, but it wasn't until it grabbed her hair with its claws that she screamed.

FIVE
OCTOBER 2003

Thomas had given Ellen the flowers anyway. He didn't know what else to do with them. After running back to his car and waiting till she and that handsome man had both left, he had walked up to the door and placed the flowers on the doormat for her to see when she came home. Crying, he had run back to his car and driven home. Now, he was sitting in his living room, staring at the wall, wondering where Ellen was and what she was doing with that guy.

Thomas looked at his phone on the table in front of him, then picked it up and found Ellen in his contacts. He called her.

"Hello?"

She sounded happy; not out of breath like they had been in the middle of something. There was a lot of noise in the background sounding like they were out somewhere. Maybe in a restaurant? Had he taken her to dinner? Had he taken her to La Petite Cuisine? Thomas swallowed hard to calm himself down. Why did she sound so happy?

Because she is with him and not you, you freak. What's not to be happy about? He is handsome, he is tall, he pleases her; you don't.

"Hello? Is there anyone there?" she asked.

Thomas opened his mouth with the intent to speak, but no words left his mouth.

"Hello? Who is this?"

Thomas breathed heavily, fighting the urge to cry.

"Who is it?" A voice asked in the background.

Probably him, probably Mr. Handsome. Do you think he is holding her hand while she is speaking to you, do you? Do you think he is looking into her eyes while caressing her hand and arm the way you dream of doing? You're a fool, Thomas. She doesn't love you. Nobody loves you.

"No one," he heard Ellen's voice reply. "Probably a wrong number. I can hear someone breathing though." She paused, then laughed. "Hello?" she asked again. "Listen, you pervert. I'm not into this kind of kinky stuff. Find someone else to breathe at."

Then she hung up.

Thomas stared at the phone as it went silent, then put it back on the table. He bit his nails while looking at the phone's display, hoping she would call him back.

"No, she does love me. I know she does," he mumbled to himself. "I'm not going to give up this easily. I'll fight for her if I have to."

Determined, Thomas rose from his chair, went into the living room, and turned on his computer. He went online and found a local florist. He ordered seven roses to be delivered to Ellen's house, one every day for a week.

That'll show her how much I love her.

As the order went through, after he paid with his credit card, he leaned back expecting to feel satisfied, but something was still very wrong. He still felt angry and so jealous. What was his Ellen doing with that creep? Suddenly, a thought struck him. What if this guy was mean to her? What if he hurt her? Thomas felt the anger rise inside of him and got up from his chair. He could not let that happen, could he? He loved her and that meant he had to protect her.

Thomas stormed out the door and jumped into his car. There weren't that many restaurants on Fanoe island. He turned on the engine and drove toward town, where most of them were, then parked the car. Knowing how much Ellen loved the place, Thomas went to La Petite Cuisine first and, just as he thought, there they were, sitting at a corner table. Thomas asked to get a table near the window so he could watch them without them seeing him. He sat down, not taking his eyes off of Ellen for even a second. He ordered a roasted duck and some wine and finally the waiter left him alone. Thomas observed the two of them as they ate and talked. Ellen laughed at something the handsome man had said. The sound of her laughter felt like knives to Thomas's heart. The handsome man put his hand on top of hers. Then he reached over and caressed her cheek. She chuckled and kissed his hand.

"Are you all right, sir?" the waiter asked.

Thomas looked up and nodded while swallowing his tears. "Yes. Yes. I just had some bad news. It'll get better."

"I brought you your wine."

"Thank you," Thomas said and forced a smile. "Just what I need."

"Very well, sir," the waiter said and poured some into Thomas's glass. Thomas tasted it and nodded, still with his eyes fixated on Ellen and the handsome man. The waiter then poured more into his glass.

"Just leave the bottle," Thomas said.

The waiter nodded before leaving. Thomas gulped down the entire glass of wine, then reached for the bottle and poured some more into it. Ellen was laughing out loud. Thomas closed his eyes. How desperately he wanted to be in that seat across from her right now. Oh, how he wanted to be the one to make her laugh like that.

Thomas opened his eyes and looked at his beautiful Ellen across the room. He didn't care for the way the handsome man was looking at her, like he wanted to devour her.

If that guy ever hurts her, I swear I'll kill him. I'll cut off his balls and feed them to him. I swear I will. Please Ellen, don't be with that guy. If you still love me, then show it to me. Show me, give me a hint.

And, just like that, she did. Just as Thomas had wished, Ellen leaned down and reached a hand into her purse and pulled out a hair tie. She pulled her hair back into a ponytail.

Thomas gasped and smiled. That was her signal. She did still love him. She knew how much he loved it when she wore her hair like that. It was her sign to him. It had to be.

Thomas lifted his glass and pretended to be saluting her, imagining that he was the man sitting across from her.

"To our love," he whispered. "A love that will last till death parts us."

SIX
NOVEMBER 2013

I kept having nightmares. I dreamed about girls being trapped in small rooms with men abusing them over and over again... Just like in the stories I had been told by the many kids we had seen on our trips to look for the missing Danish girls in Eastern Europe.

I woke up again and again with my heart pounding in my chest and tears rolling across my face. About five a.m., I couldn't sleep anymore and got out of bed. I grabbed my laptop and walked downstairs. The light was on in the kitchen and, at first, I thought I had forgotten to shut it off, but then I realized someone was in there.

"Victor?" I asked and walked closer. He was sitting with his head bent over his book, writing in his notebook like his life depended on it.

"What are you doing up, buddy? It's only five a.m."

He didn't answer or look at me, but I was used to that.

"What are you writing in the notebook?" I asked and walked closer. I looked at it from above his shoulder. It looked mostly like random numbers and letters. "What is all this, buddy?"

He didn't answer, but kept on writing. I sat down next to him with a knot in my stomach. I didn't like this; I didn't like that he wasn't sleeping properly. Was this because of me? Because I had been gone too much lately? Was this his way of telling me? I touched his hair. He froze. I removed my hand in fear that he would scream like he had before when I touched him.

"Why aren't you in bed, Vic?" I asked. "You need your sleep. You know that. You have school today, and I don't want you to be all tired and indisposed. Maybe you should go up and sleep an hour. How long have you even been down here? What made you get out of bed, huh? Did something wake you up?"

Victor turned his head and looked directly at me. I smiled. I wanted so desperately to reach out and grab him in my arms but held myself back. I didn't want to ruin the moment. "What is it, Victor? What woke you up?"

"Bats," he said. "The bats woke me up."

Then he turned his head and returned to the book.

"Bats?" I asked. "I didn't hear them."

"Of course you didn't hear them. You were asleep," he said. "I heard them. I heard them scream."

I stared at my son, not knowing what to say to him. I was thrilled he was talking to me and decided to just enjoy that.

"What are you writing?" I asked.

"Numbers."

"I see that. What kind of numbers?" I leaned over to better see but the numbers still made no sense to me. "I like the drawings there," I said, hoping he would explain to me what it was, but Victor had decided that was enough talking for now and wasn't answering me anymore. After a little while, I pulled out my laptop and opened it. I made myself some coffee and went through my many emails that had piled up while I was away. Every now and then, I glanced at Victor, enjoying just sitting there with him even if we didn't talk.

About seven, Maya came down and we had breakfast. Victor ate and got dressed and soon I had shipped both of them off to school. I answered a couple of more emails, when suddenly I heard the front door open and someone walk in. A second later, my friend Sophia peeked in through the kitchen door.

"Hello? Anyone home?" she asked.

I smiled and gave her a hug. She had her baby Alma, who was now nine months old, in her arms. She put her on the floor and kept an eye on her while she sat down. Alma quickly crawled toward the cabinets and started opening drawers. Sophia visited my house almost every day with the baby, so I made sure to keep only tablecloths and tea towels for her to pull out in the drawers she could reach. Now she was covering her head with a towel and giggling underneath.

"She does that all the time," Sophia said.

"Coffee?" I asked.

"Don't mind if I do," she said. "I want to hear everything about your trip. But I only have an hour, then I'm off to meet with my mothers' group downtown. The old theater is having an event where they're showing a film and you're allowed to bring your baby."

SEVEN
NOVEMBER 2013

Lisa was in a hurry to get everyone out of the house. She was meeting with her mothers' group downtown at the theater and didn't want to be late.

As soon as she had shipped the kids off to school and Christian had left for the office, Lisa grabbed baby Margrethe and ran upstairs with her. She changed her diaper and put her on the floor where she could play in the bedroom while Lisa got herself ready. She put on jeans and a nice shirt, but realized it had a stain on the shoulder. With a dissatisfied grunt, Lisa pulled the shirt off and found another. It wasn't as pretty as the one she wanted to wear and it made her look chubby around the waist. Lisa looked at herself in the mirror and grunted again. Christian kept telling her she was getting too skinny, but that was just something he said to make her feel better. She stared at the shirt. This wasn't at all the way she wanted to look for this event. She had planned on wearing the other one and looking amazing; that way, every other mommy in the theater would look at her with envy in their eyes, thinking *how does she do it?* It annoyed Lisa and she picked up the first shirt again to look at the stain and see if it was something she could hide somehow.

Lisa sighed. It was all over the shoulder. A big red stain. Too visible on the salmon-colored shirt that was her favorite. How infuriating. Lisa growled and threw the shirt on the bed again. The shirt was completely destroyed. Her favorite shirt ruined. She took in a couple of deep breaths to calm herself down. She had been seeing a therapist, just a couple of times, because she hadn't been able to control her anger recently. The therapist had taught her to breathe calmly and count backward. Lisa closed her eyes and tried it. It seemed to help a little. Margrethe started fussing, and Lisa reached down and picked her up in her arms. Holding her close always made her so calm and happy.

Lisa walked downstairs with Margrethe on her hip and put her in the playpen while packing the bag with diapers, pacifiers, and extra clothes in case of an accident. She let out a satisfied sigh, thinking it was going to be great just spending the day at the theater with all the other mommies. It had been years since she last went to see a film.

"Let's go, sweetie," she said and smiled at Margrethe who grinned with her two small teeth in the lower part of her mouth. She was a plump baby, but that would wear off soon enough, the doctor had said. *As soon as she starts to walk, it'll come right off.* Lisa didn't like the fact that her baby was so fat. None of her other kids had looked like this. Margrethe took more after her daddy. She even had the same nose, the poor thing. Lisa grabbed her bag, put it over her shoulder, and had just picked up Margrethe when the doorbell rang.

"Now what?" she asked and walked toward the door. She opened it with an aggressive motion. A man was standing outside the door. He looked at her.

"Yes?" she asked with irritation.

"I'm the plumber. Your husband called us and told us you had problems in the kitchen."

"My husband called you two weeks ago and you choose to show up now?" Lisa asked.

"Yes. We are very busy, Mrs. Rasmussen. You know what it's like."

"No, I don't. I'm not a plumber. How should I know what it's like?" she asked and looked at her watch.

The plumber chuckled. "No, of course you don't. It's probably a long time since you've been out in the real world, huh?" he said and smiled at Margrethe. "I mean staying home with the baby and all. Must be nice and relaxing. Getting off the rushing highway of life, right?"

I dare you to try it for one day, you creep.

"Can I come in?" he asked.

Lisa showed him inside, and he lay down under the sink in the kitchen. Lisa placed Margrethe in the playpen again.

"So how long do you think this will take?" she asked and looked at her watch again.

"It won't be long," he said as he gathered his tools, then crawled under the sink again.

Half an hour later, Lisa was getting impatient and asked again. "So, is it going to take much longer?"

"No. Not so much longer," he replied.

"Good, 'cause I have somewhere to be."

He peeked out from under the sink with a smirk. "Oh, do you now? Yeah, you must be really busy. Get a lot of stress from staying at home, do you?"

Lisa stared at the plumber, wondering if he really thought he was being funny or was he flirting in an odd way? She couldn't tell. Anyway, he annoyed her. She looked at her watch again. She had planned on going to the pharmacy before the theater. If she skipped that and left within the next fifteen minutes, she could still make it. She thought about leaving him in the house and telling him to just shut the door when he was done, but she didn't trust him. Heck, she didn't trust anyone enough to leave them alone in her house.

He'll just leave an awful mess. Look at him. Look at those dirty shoes. And he smells too. The entire house stinks already.

"So, what's the big hurry?" he asked.

"I have somewhere to be," she said. "Could you please just hurry up?"

"I'm working as fast as I can," he said. "Don't worry."

Five minutes later he pulled out from under the sink and started walking toward her. Lisa smiled. "Are you done?" she asked.

He nodded. Lisa was about to get up and pick up Margrethe.

"I'm done pulling the old pipe down," he said. "I have a new one in the car."

Lisa stared at the plumber, who walked out the door then came back with a pipe and some more tools.

"But it doesn't take long to put that in, does it?"

The plumber shrugged. "Shouldn't be more than an hour or so."

An hour?

Lisa felt like screaming. She couldn't believe this. Of all days this was happening to her, it had to be today, when she was looking forward to spending a couple of hours at the theater with her baby and friends.

The plumber smiled, then walked back into the kitchen with his tools. He threw them on the floor and left a mark in the hardwood. Lisa closed her eyes and started to count backward from one hundred. She breathed deeply and thought of positive things, like her therapist had taught her. She tried to picture the ocean, the beach, but it was too messy with all that sand. Then she pictured mountains, the beautiful Alps that they used to go skiing in during the winters before they had children. It helped a little. Her breathing calmed down, her shoulders fell back into place.

She opened her eyes and looked at Margrethe who was

fussing in the playpen, wanting to be picked up. Lisa walked to her and gave her another toy she could play with. Lisa heard the plumber drop another of his tools and closed her eyes again, but this time she didn't see any mountains or well-prepared slopes. No, this time all she saw were the marks and scratches in the dark wooden floor that they paid so much money to have put in just a few months ago. The beautiful wooden floors that she loved so much.

"Yes, sweetie, we'll be going soon. You need your nap, don't you?" Lisa said, addressing herself to Margrethe, who was getting visibly more and more frustrated with having to wait.

"Mrs. Rasmussen?" the plumber called from the kitchen.

Lisa inhaled deeply. Margrethe was crying now. "One second, sweetie," she said and handed the baby another toy. "I'll be right back."

Lisa walked with big steps toward the kitchen where the plumber was waiting for her, sitting in one of her chairs with his dirty overalls on her white seats. He smiled when he saw her.

"Yes?" she asked.

"Could I, by any chance, get a cup of coffee?" he asked.

Lisa exhaled. "I... uh," Lisa rubbed her forehead while feeling her blood boil underneath the skin. "I thought you were working?"

"Yeah, I was. But now I'm on a break. Union rules. It's a quarter to ten and that's when my break starts."

"And when does that break end if I might ask?" Lisa growled.

"In half an hour. Say, do you have a newspaper around here? I like to read while I drink my coffee."

"Of course," Lisa said with a shrill voice. "Of course you need the paper." She walked to the counter and picked the paper up and threw it on the table in front of him. "And coffee is on its way, naturally, and maybe you'd like some PASTRY to go with that? Huh?"

The plumber looked at her a little startled, then smiled and nodded. "Yeah, sure. That sounds really nice. If you have any."

Lisa walked to the cupboards and started opening all the doors, pulling out cups, plates, and spoons, which she placed on the table in front of the plumber. Then she picked up the pot of coffee from this morning and, as the plumber turned his head with a smile, she swung it through the air and smashed it into his face.

EIGHT
NOVEMBER 2013

Simone Beaumont was screaming while the animal got completely tangled up in her hair. Its claws were scratching her scalp, which hurt insanely. It was flapping its wings frantically while the most horrendous sound emerged from it. Another animal was on her back now and she screamed as she felt it bite her. It felt like there were more on her now. Teeth touching her skin, biting her. She flapped her arms in desperation, trying to knock them off. The animals screamed just as loud as her.

The light came on in the room and a voice yelled. "What on earth is going on in here?"

The animals that Simone now realized were bats, finally let go of her and flew away. Simone fell to the ground, shaking, shivering, and whimpering.

A man kneeled next to her on the other side of the fence. "You're scaring them, can't you see?" he said.

"Please... please help me," she stuttered.

"Oh, I'll help you all right. But you have to stop scaring my bats."

Simone lifted her head and looked at the man on the other side. He frightened her even more than the bats who had retired to the ceiling where they were hanging upside down, covering their small disgusting faces with their wings. There was something in this guy's eyes that freaked her out completely.

"Please help me. Please let me out," she said.

"You want to come out?" the man asked.

"Yes, please. The bats scare me. I want to go home to my family."

The man looked at her with his head tilted. He made a strange frown, then giggled very loudly. "Of course you do. Of course you want to get out. I bet you're thinking about those bats, huh? How they might bite you? How they might give you rabies? Well, not all bats have rabies. But it would kill you if they did. Did you know that they can actually transfer the disease just by getting their saliva on you? If it touches your mouth or eyes or a fresh wound. I bet you're wondering what kind of bats those are, aren't you?. Well, they're vampire bats. Do you know why they call them that? Because their food source is blood. Nasty, right? These small buddies here live solely on blood. They'll get it from any mammal in nature, including humans if they can't find anything else. Once the vampire bat locates a host, such as a sleeping mammal, it lands and approaches it on the ground. It uses thermoception to identify a warm spot on the skin to bite. They it creates a small incision with its teeth and laps up blood from the wound. Nice, right? The bats have small razor-sharp teeth; they're like a freaking barber's blade. Do you know what else they use them for?"

Simone whimpered and shook her head.

"Of course you don't," the man said. "If there is fur on the skin of the host, the common vampire bat uses its canine and cheek teeth to shave away the hairs. The bat's razor-sharp upper incisor teeth then make a deep cut. The bat's saliva, left in the victim's resulting bite wound, has a key function in feeding from the wound. The saliva contains several compounds that prolong bleeding, such as anticoagulants that inhibit blood clotting, and compounds that prevent the constriction of blood vessels near the wound. Neat, huh?"

"I... I... don't..." Simone stuttered. She was crying heavily now, wondering if she would ever see her family again.

"Of course you don't know all this. That's why I'm telling you. These bats haven't been fed in a while. I guess they are kind of hungry. I keep them here in the darkness so when I turn out the lights, they will try to go hunting. And whoops, there you are. Dinner is served."

Simone looked up at the strange man. "You're... you're going to let them feed on me?"

"That was the plan, yes. I once gave them a pig and watched how they attacked it through my infrared camera. I took some very nice pictures of it. But I've always wanted to see what it looked like when they fed on a human. You know, like real vampires. I got some pictures of you as they fed on you while you were unconscious. Don't look so worried. They didn't take much of your blood. Just a tiny bit while you slept."

"But... But you can't do this... Why? You can't keep me in here? If they're sick, I'll die."

"Hmm," the man said. "That is most unfortunate isn't it?"

"Please don't... please don't do this to me," Simone said and started hammering on the fence. "I have a family. They need me."

"Okay," the man said. "I might be able to give you a second chance."

Simone looked up. A ray of hope grew inside of her. Had her pleading helped? Did this guy have it in him to show her mercy? "You will?"

"Sure. I'm not a monster," he said and laughed. "I've had my fun. I'm getting bored with you anyway."

"So this was all a joke? You aren't going to hurt me?" Simone asked.

The man moved toward the door of the cage and unlocked it. Simone couldn't believe it. She grabbed the fence and pulled herself up. She walked toward the door that was being opened. The man smiled and held her hand so she could get out. Carefully, Simone took the first step, shaking and half-chuckling, insecurely she walked out. With a deep exhale, she watched as the man closed the door behind her and put the lock back on.

"Thank you," she said with deep relief. She looked at her arm and shoulder where the bats had bitten her in several places. There were many holes in her shirt. She pulled up the sleeve. The arm was red and swollen. She wondered if she was going to get sick. She would have to see Doctor Williamsen and get a shot when she got back home.

If she got home.

"Don't thank me yet," he said with a smile. That was when Simone realized the man was holding a rifle in his hand. She gasped with surprise.

With a wide smile, the man leaned over and pushed a button on the wall. A big door opened and Simone realized they had been in a big garage all this time. Sunlight was let in as the garage door opened and Simone laughed with relief. How had she forgotten how wonderful sunlight could be? A landscape opened up to them. The place was surrounded with elongated fields. There were horses behind a fence. How wonderful it all looked to her. And the smells. The smell of nature, of freedom. How come she had never realized how much it meant to her, how much breathing fresh air meant to her?

She took a step forward and peeked out. No other houses anywhere. She guessed they had to be in the countryside somewhere outside of Nordby. It didn't matter. As long as she got out of there, she was never coming back.

Never again. Tim, I'm coming home. Liv, Mommy's coming for you.

Simone wondered for a brief second if Liv had ever gotten

out of the car or if she was still stuck in the parking lot. No, someone must have found her. Tim must have found her and known that Simone was gone. He had to be searching for her by now. Oh, how relieved he was going to be. And what about Anthony? Had Tim taken care of him? Had he picked him up after school?

How long have I been gone? A day? A few hours? It feels like weeks.

A long, narrow, dirt road seemed to be the only way out. Simone looked at it and wished she could fly. She turned and looked at the man, then down at the rifle in his hand.

"Now what?" she said.

He lifted the rifle and looked at her through the sight. Then, he cocked it and aimed at her.

"Now, you run. Run as fast as you can."

NINE
NOVEMBER 2013

"You won't believe it."

Sophia stormed past me. It was early afternoon, and she had come back. I closed the door behind me as Sophia walked straight into the kitchen with her baby on her hip. She put Alma down, and the baby started exploring my kitchen. I found some pots and pans and a wooden spoon that she could play with.

"What's going on?"

"One of the women in my mothers' group has gone missing," Sophia said with an agitated voice.

"Gone missing, how?" I asked and signaled that she should sit down. I poured two cups of coffee and put one in front of her. My heart was pounding in my chest and, for a while, I wondered if it had any relation to the girls who had been stolen from the island back in the nineties.

Sophia gesticulated, resigned. "I don't know, Emma." She sipped her coffee. Alma was playing the pots with a grin. "She disappeared yesterday, according to her husband. When she didn't show up this morning, we called him and he told us she hadn't been home all night. That they had found her baby inside her car, screaming and crying in a parking lot downtown where she, according to the husband, had *just left her*."

"Who would leave a baby in a car?" I asked.

"I know. That's what I said. Simone would never do that. I mean she did have a difficult time with baby Liv and often spoke about how hard she thought it was, but she would never leave the baby. I can't imagine her doing such a horrible thing. The husband claims she did though. He says she has taken off, left the three of them."

I shrugged and sipped my coffee. "Could she have depression or something like that?"

"I admit, she did have tendencies. She had all the signs of postpartum depression, you know mood changes, feelings of worthlessness, hopelessness, and she was crying a lot, but heck we all do, right? We all feel that way from time to time, especially with a small baby and no sleep. I figured she was just trying to cope with it and she'd get used to it, you know?"

"Do you think she might be suicidal?" I asked.

Sophia sighed and shrugged. "I have no idea. She did mention just taking off at one point to me. She visited me at home and told me she had thought about it, not that she would ever do it, but the thought had crossed her mind. But hasn't it crossed all of our minds? I mean, I have thought about it; heck, I think about it every day, but who would take care of my six kids then, huh? What I'm trying to say is, sometimes we say stuff like that, but don't really mean it, right? I mean it might be rough from time to time, but there is so much joy to it as well, indescribable joy that nothing else in life can give us. Plus we made our bed, now we lie in it, right?"

I chuckled. She had a way of saying things, Sophia. I liked that about her. "That's what you do, yes. But still, if she might have depression, she probably doesn't think as rationally as you do. If the hopelessness gets too big, she might... well, I don't know, but I have heard stories, you know?"

"You think she has killed herself?" Sophia said with a gasp.

"No. No. I don't know her. You're the one who said she was depressed. I'm just saying that depression could drive someone to leave their child. It has happened before."

Sophia emptied her coffee cup. "Now I'm afraid you might be right."

"Do you have any idea where she might have gone? What does the husband say? Has he gone to the police?"

"He talked to them down at the station, but he is convinced that she has left them. He told me that on the phone. Apparently, she threatened to leave him the night before she disappeared. According to him, they had a big fight."

"And what do you think?" I asked, finishing my cup.

"I don't know what to think now. I'm afraid she might have done something really stupid. Come to think of it, she has been getting a lot worse the last couple of months."

I put my hand on top of Sophia's to comfort her. "Let's wait and see. Maybe she'll come home later today. Maybe she just needed a break from things to think it through. Maybe she just needed a good night's sleep in a hotel somewhere."

"I hope you're right. I really hope you are."

TEN

AUGUST 2005

Thomas was watching Ellen while she was hanging up the laundry to dry outside in the sun. He couldn't help but smile. The growing stomach made things more and more difficult for her to do, like bending down to pick up the laundry from the basket. She breathed heavily and put a hand to her stomach. Ellen was more beautiful than ever, he thought. What was it people said about pregnant women? That they glowed? Oh, yes, Ellen glowed stronger than the sun. She was as radiant as ever.

Thomas chuckled, thinking about the baby. It was a boy. They had seen it on the ultrasound. Ellen had received a picture at the hospital that she could take home. Thomas had found it going through her stuff when she was at work. She thought she could keep it a secret from him, but there were no secrets between them. He always found out somehow. He knew everything.

Thomas looked at Ellen through the binoculars and giggled. He was looking forward to this baby as much as Ellen was. Now he watched her as she walked back into the house. He could see her in the kitchen pouring herself a glass of water. Then she left for a few seconds and returned with a bouquet of flowers in her hand. Thomas chuckled again. They were his flowers. Every day for the past two years, he had sent her flowers. In the beginning, it was just one flower a day that he sent and, later, he placed one on her windscreen every morning for her to find when she drove off to work, but since she became pregnant, he had started sending more and bigger bouquets. She deserved that, he thought. Now that they were having a baby and all. It was important that she knew how much he appreciated her. It was very important in a relationship. Thomas had butterflies in his stomach when she read the card. It said the same thing every day.

Till death parts us.

Thomas giggled while watching her break the flowers and throw them in the rubbish bin. Then she sat down and cried. It was the same display every day. It was part of a game they played. She would pretend to be upset about the flowers just to make him send more. If only she knew what he had planned next.

Oh, she's going to love it. She's going to be so excited! Thomas could hardly restrain himself. He giggled and moved his feet in excitement. But he was going to wait till the baby had arrived. Then he was going to send toys, lots of toys for him. Oh, he was going to be so spoiled.

Thomas put the binoculars down and walked to the kitchen of the flat he had rented across the road from Ellen's house. He had lost his job at the port because he stopped showing up, but that didn't matter. He had his unemployment benefit from the government, and that was enough for him to pay the rent for this studio and the little else he needed. He had practically no furniture, but he didn't need that either. As long as he could be close to his beloved, he could live on the street for all he cared.

He made himself a sandwich and ate it while looking out the window, keeping an eye on her, in case she left. He looked at his watch while chewing. Her appointment with Doctor

Williamsen wasn't until two o'clock. She would probably have to stop for gas on the way, as she was running low, so she would need to go ten minutes before. He still had time to finish his lunch. He picked up the binoculars and watched as Ellen prepared herself to go out. She put on makeup and found a new maternity dress in the wardrobe. After the doctor's appointment she was going to meet up with a friend for a cup of coffee. Thomas was looking forward to seeing the friend again. It had been months since they had last seen her.

Thomas chewed the ham sandwich and washed it down with a soda. While Ellen went to the bathroom, Thomas ran to the hallway and grabbed his jacket. When he was back in the window, Ellen was putting on her jacket as well. He looked at his watch.

Right on time, sweetheart. As always.

Thomas put the binoculars in the inside pocket of his jacket, then stormed down the stairs and jumped into his car where he waited for Ellen to leave the house and get into hers.

ELEVEN
NOVEMBER 2013

"I'm running for city council."

Christian dropped his fork into the spaghetti and meat sauce. "You're what?"

Lisa sat up straight in her chair. Out of the corner of her eye she could still see the small carpet she had put on the kitchen floor to cover up the marks made by the plumber's tools. She felt a breath of satisfaction and looked down at the meat sauce on her plate. He had gotten what he deserved, the bastard. Coming here and ruining her day and her floors. Making her be late for her appointment with her friends. "You heard me," she said.

Christian burst into laughter. "You're kidding, right?"

Lisa didn't laugh. She looked at her husband, sensing the furor rising in her once again. She inhaled deeply. "No, *sweetheart*. I'm not kidding. I'm dead serious."

Christian's smile froze. "You're serious? But... but Lisa. How? Why? The election is in two weeks. Nobody knows you. Is it even possible to announce your candidacy this late? I don't think it is. You're not even a member of a political party."

"I'll run as nonattached. People will like that. Something different. Someone with new thoughts and ideas."

"Mom," Amalie said. "What are you even talking about?"

"I'm talking about this city. I walked through it today with Margrethe in the pram and there is rubbish everywhere. I mean people are such disgusting pigs. You wouldn't believe it. Not to mention how it looks down by the port. Somebody has to do something around here and it might as well be me." Lisa picked up her fork and spoon and swirled the spaghetti into a perfect-sized ball and ate it. She had really outdone herself with the sauce this time. Christian had said so himself when they had started eating. The kids had agreed. Lisa told them she had used her secret recipe.

Christian stared at her like she had gone mad.

"Eat your dinner, sweetheart," Lisa chirped. "It's getting cold."

"So you're really doing this, Mom?" Amalie asked.

"Yes. Tomorrow I'm going to City Hall and let them know. I sense I can make a big difference."

"But what about Margrethe?" Christian asked.

"I'll take her with me. I'm thinking I'll have her on the pictures on the poster too. Makes me look trustworthy, don't you think? Appealing to the mothers."

"You're going to be on a poster?" Amalie said with a frown. Then she rolled her eyes. "That is so embarrassing."

"Well, if I'm not on a poster, how will people know to vote for me?" Lisa asked. She looked at Jacob who had been quiet during the entire dinner. He had hardly eaten. "Jacob, eat your dinner," she said.

"I called the plumber today," Christian said. "To hear what was going on and when they intended to send someone out here."

Lisa stopped chewing and looked up. "Oh, and what did they say?"

"They said they already sent a guy. They said they sent him this morning. No one was here, right?"

"No. I mean, I was at the theater until lunch and then we went to a café to eat, so someone might have come and gone without me knowing it."

"That's what I thought. Typical. Now I have to reschedule. I can't believe this small thing can cause me this much trouble."

"Well, do whatever you need to do, honey," Lisa said and put her hand on top of Christian's. In her mind, she planned on giving him a blow job when the kids were in bed. It was important to keep him satisfied in order to hold on to him. Intercourse didn't appeal to her lately.

"More sauce?"

"Yes, please. It is really good," he said and tapped his stomach. "I need to watch my weight. I tell you. With your cooking lately, I'm getting fat."

"Oh, you're not fat," Lisa said and poured more meat sauce over his spaghetti. "Here."

"Thanks."

Jacob looked up from his plate. "The new freezer arrived today."

"What?" Christian said and looked at Lisa. "You bought another freezer? Do we really need that?"

"It's just for the basement. Mr. Moerch from the farm outside of town, the one on Rindbyvej, has just slaughtered one of his cows and he promised me a lot of meat for practically no money. I couldn't refuse that offer."

Christian looked at Lisa, stunned. "But how much was the freezer? I mean what's the idea of getting a lot of cheap meat if we have to buy an expensive freezer to contain it?"

"It was a bargain," Lisa said with a smile. "Don't worry. More meat sauce?"

TWELVE
NOVEMBER 2013

Simone was running. The bumpy dirt road made it difficult for her in her high-heeled boots and soon, she stumbled and fell with her face in the mud. Panting, she sprang to her feet again. She turned her head to look behind her and saw the man standing outside the garage with the rifle still pointed at her. She gasped as she heard it go off. Then she ran faster.

Thinking it would make it more difficult for the man to hit her she started zigzagging. Another shot was fired and Simone felt a pain in her right leg. She screamed and fell to the ground, face first. The pain was excruciating, yet she managed to pull herself up and, with the leg dragging behind her, she moved forward, panting, crying, and whimpering in pain.

"I'm coming, Liv. I'm coming home, Tim," she cried.

Simone turned her head and saw the man stare at her. He had lowered the rifle and was watching her like he wanted to see if she would fall again. Simone pulled all of her strength together and forced herself to start running again, forgetting the pain in her leg.

Come on legs, run. Run. Just make it to the end of the road, and you're free. Keep moving. Don't stop and let him hit you again. Keep moving.

Simone burst into a scream as another shot was fired, but missed her and hit a tree not far from her. She cried but didn't stop moving. She forced herself to move forward and soon fear made her forget the pain, press through it, and start running again. She was panting and moaning, while burning with fear.

Please don't let him hit me again. Please don't. Oh, God, stop him; blur his vision, make him stop, don't let him...

Another shot scattered the icy air and Simone felt a pain in her shoulder. She screamed and fell forward to her knees.

Keep running. You've got to keep moving.

She looked back over her shoulder and saw the man had started moving closer. He was walking with the rifle in his arms. Simone held a hand to her shoulder. Blood was gushing down her arm and painting her shirt.

Come on, Simone. Pull yourself up. He will kill you. Do it for Liv. Do it for Anthony. They need you. You can't let him get to you. You can't let him kill you. Don't let him get any closer. This is it. This is the moment. Run! For Pete's sake, just run.

Moaning heavily in pain, Simone managed to pull herself up from the mud yet another time. She wasn't able to run anymore, but she could still walk, dragging her leg after her.

"You can't catch me, I'm the gingerbread man," she heard the man say, not far behind her. Then he laughed. "Stop, stop. I want to eat you," he said with a shrill voice.

Another shot scattered through the air and a huge flock of birds took off from a treetop. The shot missed her again. Simone felt relief flood through her body when she suddenly spotted the big road in the distance. She knew this road. It was the road leading to town. She spotted a car in the far distance and screamed.

"HEEEELLLP!"

But the car passed her without even slowing down.

"Please help me," she cried, reaching out her hand trying to wave and make them come back.

She could hear the man's voice behind her. He was getting closer now. She tried to walk faster.

Come on. Just a few more yards and you're there, Simone. Come on. You can make it. You're so close now. Don't give up, don't give up now.

Simone heard the sound of another car approaching in the distance. She turned and saw it coming toward her. She lifted her arm and waved and screamed.

"HEEEELP! HEEELP ME!"

But the road was still too far away for the driver to see her. She tried to run, but the pain was too excruciating. She cried as she heard another shot go off and felt a pain in her back. The hit made her fall into the mud.

"Please don't... please don't kill me."

She couldn't get up anymore. She heard steps coming up from behind her and saw the man's boots in the dirt next to her face. Then she heard his voice. He was talking like cartoon characters, making different voices.

"You won't eat me, will you? said the gingerbread man. Of course not, said the fox. I just want to help."

The man giggled, then lifted the rifle and pointed it at her face.

"I'll save you. Just jump onto my nose and I'll help you get to the other side."

Simone's body was shaking heavily as she stared into the barrel of the rifle. She wanted to speak, to say something, to call him a creep, a bastard, but no words left her mouth. Only spurting and gasping as the blood overflowed her mouth and ran across her lips.

THIRTEEN
NOVEMBER 2013

I couldn't stop thinking about the missing woman all evening and night. I lay awake in my bed for hours thinking about the poor woman and whether she was out there somewhere, wandering around depressed and suicidal. I didn't like it one bit. Finally, I fell asleep about two o'clock and had a horrible nightmare. I woke up at four to the sound of wailing sirens, a very unusual sound on our small island.

I got up and looked out the window. I spotted one of the island's police cars driving toward the beach, not far from my house. I felt a knot in my stomach and got dressed. In the hallway, I met Maya. She was still half asleep.

"What's going on, Mom?"

"Nothing, sweetie. I just saw a police car go down to the beach. I'm going down there to see if they need any help. Just go back to bed. It's probably nothing."

"Then why are you going? To see Officer Morten?"

"Just go back to sleep," I said, knowing she was partially right. I knew he was working the night shift and I wanted to see him again. Also I was curious as to what was going on.

I stormed outside and bumped into Jack in the street. He

blushed when he saw me. "I... I guess y-you're curious too, huh?" he said, stuttering.

I smiled and gave him a hug. We started walking toward the beach. "The sirens woke me up. I thought I might as well go down and see if they needed any help. I know there is only one man on duty at this time of night, and he might need a hand," I said, trying to explain that I wasn't one of those horrible persons who stopped to look at traffic accidents.

"Me too," Jack said. "Any idea what is going on?"

I shook my head. We passed the small ice cream shop at the entrance to the public access to the beach. It was now closed for the winter and looked old and abandoned. I spotted the police car parked farther down and saw Officer Morten talking to someone, a young teenager who looked very upset. My heart skipped a beat when Officer Morten turned his head to look at us. His eyes lit up, but he remained serious. I knew by the look on his face that this was bad.

He said something to the teenager, then approached us. "What's going on?" I asked.

Officer Morten sighed. "The kid says he saw a car drive into the ocean, but we can't see a damn thing in this darkness. If I had more flashlights, we could all go down there and search."

"I... I have two at my house," Jack said. "I'll go get them."

"Great. I have one in my car too," Officer Morten said.

"What was he even doing down here?" I asked, as we started running toward the ocean.

"Apparently, he has a broken heart and couldn't sleep. He lives right up the street. He was sitting on the sand when the car came driving down the beach and continued into the ocean. It had no lights on, he said."

Officer Morten lit his flashlight and we stopped. I could see nothing but the dark ocean as far as the eye could see. "There doesn't seem to be anything."

After a few minutes I spotted Jack come running across the

wide beach. He handed me a flashlight, and we started scanning the area. Still no trace. I turned my flashlight on and lit up the sand.

"Here, guys. Over here," I said.

I pointed the flashlight on the sand. "See here. That looks like it was made by tires, if I'm not mistaken."

"And they continue into the water," Officer Morten said with a moan.

"The kid was right," I said and followed the tracks with my flashlight into the water, then lit up the water. The light hit what looked like the top of a car.

"There it is," Officer Morten said and pulled off his shirt. He jumped into the water and started swimming toward it. With fast-beating hearts, Jack and I made sure our flashlights stayed on the car so he could see. Officer Morten dove into the water and disappeared for a few seconds.

"There's someone in there!" he yelled, as he emerged from the water again.

Without thinking, Jack pulled off his shirt and jumped in as well.

FOURTEEN
NOVEMBER 2013

Jack and Officer Morten managed to pull a body out of the car and drag it up on the beach. With my heart pounding in my chest, I watched as they placed her lifeless body on the sand. Officer Morten bent over her.

"She's dead," he said.

"Drowned?" I said, dreading that we had come too late, fearing that we had been close to saving her, if only we had been earlier.

"No," Morten said. He turned her body around. "Look at this," he said and pointed at wounds in her back, shoulder, and leg.

"Oh, my God. That looks like gunshots. Has she been shot?" I asked and looked at Jack who was sitting in the sand, catching his breath from swimming while carrying the woman's body.

"I'm afraid so," Morten said. "Several times." He sighed and rose to his legs. "Poor Tim. He's gonna be devastated."

"You know her?" I asked.

"Yes. Tim is my colleague."

"He's a police officer?"

"Yes. This is his wife. Simone. They just had a baby nine months ago. Their second child. Simone disappeared yesterday and left her baby in the car. They had been in a fight the night before, he told us. We all thought she would come back, you know?"

My heart dropped. I nodded. "I know. You weren't the only ones."

With another deep sigh, Officer Morten grabbed his phone and looked at me. "I better call for help. We'll need lots of it. The forensic team from Copenhagen, the whole lot. This might be a long night. I'll also have to tell Tim somehow."

I smiled and put a hand on his shoulder.

"You go home and get your sleep," he said to me and Jack. "I'll swing by tomorrow and take your statements for the report."

"Will you be all right?" I asked, then felt stupid. Of course he would. It was his job. But still. It wasn't something you just got used to, was it? Especially not when it was a colleague who was affected by this.

"I'll be okay, I'm not the one to worry about," Morten said and put the phone to his ear. "I'll call in for more officers to help me."

I looked at Jack, and we started walking back in silence. As we reached my house, we looked at each other. "What a night, huh?" I said. "Do you want to come in and get a cup of coffee? I have a feeling neither of us is getting anymore sleep tonight."

"I better go back to make sure my sister is all right. She wakes up several times at night. If I'm not there, she'll be scared."

"Of course. Me too. I mean my kids need me too. So... I guess... I'll see you later," I said.

Jack nodded. I gave him a hug and watched him walk back to his house with his head slightly bent. He was a handsome guy, but just didn't know it. I liked that about him. I had liked him for a long time, but with him, everything was just too complicated. He was taking care of his sister, and that made it almost impossible for him to be in a relationship. It was like he had given up on the hope of ever having one.

I shrugged and walked inside. I poured myself a glass of milk and tried to fall asleep, but thoughts of the woman and her husband and their poor children kept me awake. Who had shot her? And how was it even possible for her to drive her car into the ocean? Was she trying to get help? Maybe she had managed to escape whoever hurt her somehow and then died behind the wheel driving into the ocean? I thought about Sophia and how sad she was going to be, losing one of her friends like this.

It was almost five in the morning before I finally fell asleep.

FIFTEEN
NOVEMBER 2013

Lisa took Margrethe on her hip and walked inside City Hall. The red brick building looked charming from the outside, but Lisa was disappointed to learn that the decor inside left a lot to be desired.

"Yet another thing I can help change," she chirped and walked toward the reception desk. The clerk behind the counter didn't even look up when she approached him. She cleared her throat. He still didn't look up from his book. She cleared her throat louder. Finally, he lifted his eyes and looked at her.

"Yes? What do you want?"

"What do I want?"

Doesn't he know whom he is talking to? Another thing about to change once Mrs. Rasmussen takes over.

"Yes. What do you want?" he repeated, annoyed.

"Is that a way to address a person entering City Hall, the heart of the town?" Lisa asked.

He sighed. "I'm kind of busy. Could you please just tell me if there is anything I can help you with?"

Lisa smiled. "Now that's better. Young man, I'm here to

sign up for the coming election."

"You're what?"

"I wish to be elected for city council."

"You're a little late, lady," the young man said. "The election is in two weeks."

"I know when the election takes place, and I want to be in it. Now please just tell me where I sign up with my name."

The clerk shrugged. "Well, I can put your name on the list. There aren't that many candidates, so I guess we could add another name. But I have to tell you, the last eight years there haven't been any replacements in the council. They sit pretty heavily in their seats once they've gotten a hold of them."

"Well, I guess that's about to change then," Lisa said.

The clerk shrugged. "Suit yourself, lady. I'm just telling you, it's a waste of time. The council members already sitting there are all up for reelection. So, unless one of them moves away or dies or something..."

"Well, that can be arranged."

"Excuse me?"

Lisa shook her head with a grin. "Nothing. I'm just joking around with you. Now where do I sign?"

The clerk passed a piece of paper to her on the counter. "Right here, here, and on the last page."

Lisa found her lucky pen in her purse and, while still holding Margrethe in her other arm, she signed the papers. "There you go. Now Mommy's all signed up."

She handed the papers back to the clerk. He looked at them. "Well, you're all set to go. Good luck, lady."

"Well, thank you." Lisa looked at her baby and tickled her tummy. Margrethe whined in joy. "Mommy's gonna make a lot of changes in here, isn't she? You betcha. Yes, she is."

"Don't get your hopes up too high," the clerk mumbled.

Lisa froze and looked at him. "What was that?"

He shook his head. "Nothing. I just said to not get your

hopes up too high. I mean even if you did get elected, there really isn't much being changed around here. Everything pretty much stays the same."

"*If* I get elected? What is that supposed to mean?" Lisa asked very loudly. "I intend to get elected and then I'm gonna MAKE things happen around here. You HEAR me?"

The clerk stared at her with wide-open eyes, completely startled.

"Don't forget to blink," Lisa said with her most gentle smile and turned around. Just as she was about to leave City Hall, she turned and looked at him again.

"Take a good look at my face," she said. "You'll be seeing a lot more of it in the future."

SIXTEEN
OCTOBER 2009

Ellen was crying again. Thomas was watching her through his binoculars while drinking a canned soda. She had been crying a lot lately and it hurt him so deeply to see her like this.

The handsome man entered the kitchen, and they started arguing again. The kids were in the garden running after each other, screaming. Ellen was shaking her head and gesticulating. Thomas took another bite of his ham sandwich and drank more soda. It was the same day after day now. Them fighting, the kids crying and screaming.

Thomas shook his head. It was hard to see his beloved in this much distress. The husband was hardly ever home anymore and, when he was, they were constantly fighting. Thomas sighed and drank again. He wanted so badly to help Ellen out, but there was no way her husband could ever know about them. This was the way Ellen wanted it. She had to keep their relationship a secret because she had a family to think of. Thomas understood that. But he never stopped sending her flowers, even if he knew it was often the subject of their many discussions. And so were the letters. Thomas had found a new way of communicating with his beloved. While he was in her house, when she was off at work, he would place notes and letters in her drawers and wardrobes, sometimes just a sticky note on her clothes or the wall, telling her how deeply he loved her. He knew it was risky, but his beloved needed his encouragement. She needed to know she was loved.

Thomas watched the husband in the kitchen. He was standing by the door, obviously yelling at Ellen while she was sitting in a chair, her hands folded in her lap. She was crying and it infuriated Thomas to see her like this. He clenched his fist.

If he ever hurts her, I swear to God I'm gonna...

The husband was gesticulating wildly, and Ellen hid her face between her hands. Thomas restrained himself. He wanted so badly to just run over there and beat the crap out of him.

The bastard. He didn't know how lucky he was to wake up to this woman every day.

But he couldn't know about them. The husband could never know. It would destroy everything. And, even if it was hard, Thomas respected Ellen's wish to keep their relationship a secret. He had to. Instead, he always kept an eye on Ellen to make sure she was safe. It was his job to protect her.

Thomas turned the binoculars to look at the children playing in the garden. The oldest, Frederik, was on the swings while the youngest, Gerda, was playing with a jump rope. Thomas chuckled. How he adored those two munchkins. He often talked to them on the playground nearby where they came every afternoon with their nanny and, just as often, he had given them sweets. Gerda was always so sweet and smiling, taking the sweets willingly right away, while Frederik had been more reserved the first time. When Thomas had told them he knew their mother well, Frederik had loosened up a little and taken the gummy bears. Thomas had really gotten close to them lately and started giving them new toys now and then, by simply placing them on their beds while he was in the house.

The husband hadn't been too happy about Thomas's small gifts but Ellen loved them. Thomas knew she did. She would tell him in her own way. Through signals like pulling the curtains or by putting the newspaper on top of the rubbish bin, so when he opened the lid to go through it, he would see an article where she had circled something. Ellen and Thomas had a love language of their own and a way of communicating that no one else in the world would ever understand or know.

Thomas heard the husband yell and turned to look into the kitchen again. The handsome husband was still yelling and stomping his feet. Ellen was crying heavily now. Thomas inhaled deeply trying to calm himself down. Then he turned to look at the kids again only to realize that Gerda had managed to somehow climb the big tree in their garden and tied the jump rope around a branch. Thomas gasped as he watched her jump and accidentally get the rope around her neck. With a shriek, he turned to look at Ellen and the husband who were still fighting, then back at the girl who was struggling with the rope around her neck, while Frederik was still on the swings, not seeing anything.

Thomas threw the binoculars on the floor and stormed out of the door.

SEVENTEEN
NOVEMBER 2013

Officer Morten Bredballe stopped by late in the afternoon the next day. The kids had just gotten home from school and had eaten their freshly baked buns. Victor had gone into the garden to play while Maya was upstairs doing her homework, at least I hoped she was.

I invited him inside the kitchen and poured him a cup of coffee.

He chuckled. "Do I look that bad, huh?"

"Well, you look like you could use a cup. Let's just leave it at that," I said and poured myself a cup. He took my statement for the report. It didn't take long. When he was done, he asked for another cup of coffee. I poured him one and placed the basket of buns on the table.

"Want one?"

"Yes, please," he said with a sigh. "That would be great. It's been a long night and an even longer day. Can't remember when I last ate."

I cut one open and handed it to him. He buttered it and started eating it. "Mmm, these are really good," he moaned and sipped the coffee. "Thanks. I really needed this. This day has been hell. You have no idea."

"So, did you tell the family?"

Morten stopped chewing and nodded. "That was the worst part, Emma; I tell you, it was so hard."

"How did he take it?" I asked and buttered a bun for myself even if it was my fourth this afternoon.

"He was in deep shock, still is. He couldn't believe it and started blaming himself for not having looked for her yesterday. He kept saying that he had thought she was just punishing him for their fight and that she would be back. He had never imagined this happening to her."

"Does he need anything? I could cook for him and leave enough in the freezer for a couple of days so he wouldn't have to think about cooking," I said.

"Someone already suggested doing the same, so I don't think there will be any need for that."

I nodded pensively and sipped my coffee. "Does he need something else maybe? Someone to take the kids for a while? I could easily have them here at the house for a couple of days, if he needed it. I mean there have to be a lot of things for him to do now, like arrange the funeral and all."

"I'll let him know. The funeral won't be for a while though, because the forensic techs are working on her and the body won't be released for quite some time."

"No, of course not. What have they come up with so far?" I asked. "If you can talk about it, that is."

"There is going to be a press conference later today where the details are all going to be revealed, so there is no harm in me telling you. She was shot several times just as we suspected. The forensic techs furthermore found animal bites on her body. Mostly on her shoulder, arm, and back."

"Animal bites? What kind of animal?" I asked and finished

my bun. I grabbed another one and buttered it. "More?" I asked Officer Morten.

"Well, one more then. They're so good," he said with a smile.

"You need it more than I do," I said and pushed the butter toward him so he could reach it.

He buttered his bun and took a bite.

"So what kind of animal are we talking about? Do they even know at this point?" I asked.

Officer Morten leaned over and swallowed before he spoke. "That's the strange thing. It seems it's bats. Bites from a bat all over her arm and back."

I almost spurted out my coffee. "Bats?" I asked, thinking about Victor who had been awake the other night because he claimed to have heard bats screaming.

"Yes, bats."

"But they eat insects, don't they?"

"Well, yes, but apparently there are different kinds of bats. This type is named the vampire bat because it feeds on blood from mammals. They bite down through the skin and drink the blood that runs from the wound."

I suddenly lost my appetite and put the bun down. "Are you kidding me? Like real vampires?"

"That's where the myth started, I guess. Anyway, as you might understand, we are looking for anyone who might have bats as pets."

"Hmm," I said.

"What?"

"Well, my son Victor was awake the other night. He told me he had heard bats screaming. Maybe you're looking for someone not so far away from here?"

Officer Morten ate and nodded. "That sounds like something we might have to look into."

I nodded, thinking it freaked me out a little to think that this bat-loving killer could be anywhere close to us. But wouldn't we have heard the shots if he was anywhere close? I shook my head. "But again, it's Victor. It might have been a very vivid dream or one of his strange visions. As I've told you before, sometimes he sees and hears things the rest of us don't. Do you have any idea why the killer chose this girl?"

"No. It might be random. We believe she was taken at the parking lot where we found the car and the child. Tim told us she had felt like she had been watched for a couple of days before she disappeared, so the killer might have observed her for some time before taking her. There is a team from Copenhagen who has joined us in the investigation. They will be going over Simone's whereabouts for the past few days to see if the killer shows up on any surveillance cameras or if anyone has seen him."

"Sounds like the killer planned this," I said, finishing my bun after all. I sipped my coffee and looked at Officer Morten. He looked exhausted. He wasn't the most handsome man, but there was something about him I really liked: a gentleness, a sweetness. And he was so simple. Divorced with a teenage daughter. That was all. We had grown very close on our trips to Eastern Europe together the past many months, and I truly enjoyed his company. We never got around to having the date we discussed, there simply hadn't been time for it.

"But there is more," Officer Morten said.

"I had a feeling there would be," I said and finished my coffee. I offered him more, but he refused.

"Have to get back soon," he said. Then he exhaled. "There has been another disappearance on the island."

I looked at him. "What?"

"We don't know if it is related, but this morning we were contacted by Nordby VVS, you know the plumbing company. They told us one of their young plumbers had vanished. They had sent him on the road to a couple of assignments yesterday but he never showed up. The lorry was found parked downtown at a parking place behind the old theater, but there was no sign of the plumber. We have no idea if it is related; he might have just gone on a bender. He was known to be a drunk, but we have to treat it as though it is related."

"Of course you do."

Officer Morten got up from his chair with a sigh. "Well, I'd better get going. I have to finish my report before I can finally go home and have a few hours of sleep."

I escorted him out. I opened the door and held it for him while he put on his jacket. He was about to walk out, when he suddenly hesitated. I looked at him. He looked up and our eyes locked for a few seconds. Then he leaned forward and grabbed me in his arms and hugged me. I was taken completely by surprise by this gesture, but enjoyed it. He held me tight for a few seconds more, then whispered in my ear, "I really like you, Emma. I hate that we only see each other when bad things happen. I want to make good memories with you."

I was startled. Speechless. "I... uh... well..."

He looked into my eyes. "I have baffled you, haven't I?"

"Slightly... but not in a bad way," I said. "I like being baffled."

Officer Morten chuckled. "Life is short, you know?"

I smiled. "Life is short and one should be baffled every now and then."

Officer Morten nodded and put on his police cap. "I'll pick you up tomorrow night then. Would about seven be all right?"

EIGHTEEN
NOVEMBER 2013

Susanne Arnholm was breastfeeding. Her nipples were sore and had been for weeks now. Mastitis, inflammation of the breast tissue, her doctor had said. He gave her some antibiotics and told her that it might be time to stop breastfeeding. But Susanne didn't want to. She loved breastfeeding her baby Malthe. With her first child, Christine, she had breastfed until the child was almost four years old. She would have continued, but had to stop since she was almost due with Malthe, and he was going to take over.

Susanne closed her eyes while Malthe sucked on her sore nipples. They were red and swollen and Susanne had a slight fever because of the infection. Still, she continued through the pain... For the child's sake. Everybody knew breast milk was by far the best for a child. No other milk contained the combination of nutrients that a child needed like a mother's own milk.

She looked down at Malthe who sucked contentedly. As she looked up at her friends at the table, she received a couple of disapproving looks from other guests in the café, but Susanne didn't care. She was used to people staring, even if she never understood why anyone would be appalled by someone breastfeeding. It was, after all, the most natural thing in the world. The other women in her mothers' group all went aside or hid the baby and breast under a blanket like they were ashamed of breastfeeding in public. It had gotten worse in the last six months, ever since some restaurants and cafés had thrown women out for breastfeeding in public. It had led to a demonstration in Copenhagen that Susanne had taken part in. She hated the way it was now, something she had to hide or be ashamed of. So, Susanne went in the opposite direction. She hid nothing from anyone. She didn't cover up with a blanket. When her nine-month-old baby was hungry, she simply pulled up her shirt and started feeding him, no matter where she was. If people stared at her bare breast, then she let them. If people were appalled, then she let them be. If she was asked to leave by a waiter, she told them she wouldn't and that they'd have to call the police if they wanted to throw her out. And then she threatened to write bad things about the place on Facebook telling everybody that they were against women breastfeeding; that usually shut them up because most cafés lived very well off of the many mothers' groups that came in for brunch.

"Susanne, I can see your nipple," one of the women in her mothers' group named Lisa said.

Susanne shrugged. "So what?"

"Well... at least cover up a little bit with your shirt. I can practically see the entire breast."

"Then don't look," Susanne said.

Lisa growled and ate her salad. Susanne really didn't like Lisa much. She was so uptight. And now she had told them that she was running for the city council. Susanne had stared at her and tried hard not to laugh. At least it had lightened up the mood in the mothers' group a little. They had all been really down since Simone disappeared, and this morning they had heard that she had been found shot in a car in the ocean. It was all very strange and creepy. Susanne wasn't scared because she was certain Simone's husband did it.

"He fits the profile. He is the typical power-tripping police officer," she had stated when the rest of the group had told her she was crazy for making such a statement.

"Tim loved her," Sophia had said. Sophia Six Kids, as Susanne secretly had named her, because she was alone with six children, all with different fathers. She was by far Susanne's favorite in the group.

"Yeah, but that just gives him a motive, doesn't it? I mean they had a big fight the night before, didn't they? And then she is suddenly gone the next day? Looks a little suspicious to me."

The group had agreed to disagree. They did that a lot. Now Lisa was looking disapprovingly at Susanne's breast while Malthe finished his meal.

"I really don't understand why you don't just introduce him to the bottle," Lisa grumbled. "Margrethe never slept better than since I started giving her a bottle."

"Well, I'm not going to, so live with it," Susanne said.

Susanne was sweating heavily because of the pain. She wiped her forehead with a napkin. She closed her eyes for a second while the other women, including the always very quiet Nora, talked about Lisa's new upcoming career.

"I'll definitely vote for you," Sophia stated.

The rest nodded. Lisa looked smug. It annoyed Susanne. She looked away. Her eyes met with those of a man sitting across the room at a table by the window. She thought she had seen his face before and smiled as she would smile to an acquaintance she met in the street or at the supermarket.

He smiled back.

NINETEEN
OCTOBER 2009

Oh, my God, she's going to be choked!

Thomas ran across the street and stormed into the garden through the back opening in the fence. He ran to the tree where Gerda was hanging lifelessly from the branch. Her face had turned purple, and she wasn't moving.

Thomas gasped, then climbed the tree and reached down to grab her by the shoulder and pulled her back up into the tree.

"Please breathe; please don't be dead," he said, panting while untying the rope from around her throat. Gerda's older brother had now realized something was going on and approached the tree.

Thomas looked at the young girl in his hands while his heart was racing in his chest. Everything inside of him was screaming.

Please don't die; please don't.

He leaned over her and listened, then put his fingers on her wrist to feel for a pulse. He didn't find any and she wasn't breathing.

"What's happening?" Frederik asked with a shivering voice.

"Get your mom and dad," Thomas yelled. "Go get your parents. Now."

Frederik disappeared and Thomas put Gerda over his shoulder and carefully carried her down. He placed her in the grass, then opened her mouth and breathed in. Then he pressed her chest carefully, so as to not break any of her ribs.

"Come on, Gerda. Come on, sweetheart. Wake up. Breathe."

When nothing happened, he leaned over and breathed into her mouth again, then pressed on her chest again. Finally, something happened. Gerda spurted and coughed. Her legs and arms moved in what looked like spasms. Thomas was crying heavily, tears rolling across his face. Voices emerged from the house. Frederik was running toward them; Ellen and her handsome husband following him.

"What's going on?" Ellen screamed.

Thomas looked up and his eyes met hers. Oh, how he loved those deep blue eyes that he had admired for so long.

"Who are you?" she asked.

"I... I..." Thomas stuttered. He looked down at Gerda who was still coughing.

Ellen took her in her arms. "Are you all right, sweetie?" Ellen looked at her handsome husband. "We need to call for an ambulance. Please hurry up." Then she looked at Thomas again.

"What happened?"

"She... she got the jump rope around her throat... up in the tree. I saw it and got her down."

Ellen put a hand to her chest. "Oh, dear God."

"She was hanging from the tree over there," Thomas continued and pointed. The jump rope was still tied to the branch.

Ellen shrieked and held her daughter closer. She was so fragile and tender at that moment. Thomas could never have loved her more. "I... I climbed up there and managed to get her down. She wasn't breathing..."

Thomas felt the husband's hand on his shoulder. He had talked to the emergency dispatcher and put the phone in his pocket. "How can we ever thank you?" he said.

"Well... I... it was nothing, really." Thomas rose to his feet. His eyes avoided Ellen's. This was a very uncomfortable situation. "I'd better... I should go."

"Wait," Ellen said.

Thomas stopped. Ellen looked at him. Their eyes locked. "Haven't I seen you before?"

"Well... I... live nearby."

Suddenly her facial expression changed. "It's you, isn't it?"

Her husband looked at Thomas. "What are you saying, Ellen?" he asked.

"It's him. I know it's him."

The husband took a step closer to Thomas. "You? You're the one who sends the flowers? You're the one who breaks into our house and posts letters and places toys in our children's room? You're the reason we've had to change the locks six times in the last few years?"

Thomas looked down. He didn't answer.

"What kind of a creep are you?" The husband snorted.

Thomas looked at Ellen, longing for some sort of recognition of their mutual love, of the many secrets they had shared over the years.

She shook her head heavily. "Listen. We are extremely grateful for what you have done for our daughter," she said, but was interrupted by her husband.

"No. No. This guy only saw what happened because he was spying on us, on our children. He is a creep, Ellen. He needs to be locked away."

Thomas started to back up slowly. "I... I should..."

"No," Frederik said. "Don't be mean to him."

His parents looked at him.

"I know him," he continued. "His name is Thomas, and he

is really nice. He saved Gerda's life. He gives us sweets at the playground."

In the distance, Thomas heard sirens blaring and soon an ambulance drove into the driveway.

"Do you mean to say that this creep has been approaching you and Gerda at the playground?" The handsome man said with a furious voice. "That's it, mister," he said and lifted his clenched fist. "You leave my family alone, or I swear to God..."

"Where is the patient?" A voice interrupted them. "Is that the girl?"

Ellen nodded while the husband forgot all about Thomas and turned to look at Gerda. Thomas slowly backed up, and while everybody else was busy attending the girl, he snuck out of the garden and ran back to his flat. For the rest of the day, he sat in the window, his hands shaking so badly he could hardly hold the binoculars still.

TWENTY
NOVEMBER 2013

Lisa was having a busy day. All morning, she was having photos taken for the posters, and then she needed to get a new outfit for her upcoming campaign. She went for a nice dress, not too colorful, but in a nice dim beige, making her look trustworthy, yet motherly. She had Margrethe on her hip in some of the pictures and was alone in others.

Afterward, she was off to enjoy a late lunch with her friends in her mothers' group before she had her nails done at that small new place downtown.

At home, she cooked enough food for an army, then wrapped it all up and put it in boxes before she headed over to Tim Beaumont's house. She rang the doorbell and he opened the door. His eyes were red and swollen.

"I cooked for you," she said and stormed past him into the kitchen where she unpacked all her boxes and bags. "There should be enough to eat for a long, long time," she said. "All you have to do is heat it."

"It's really nice of you, Lisa," Tim said with a heavy voice. He sat down on a chair and stared at the floor. Lisa felt sorry for him. She had always liked Simone and was sad that she was gone.

"It's the least I can do. I had all this meat in my freezer anyway, so I'm just glad to use it to help you. Here, this is for tonight. It's a stew."

Tim nodded. "Thanks. The kids will probably love it. I don't seem to have any appetite lately."

"Well, that's only natural, Tim. Give it time, okay?"

"You're always so good to talk to, Lisa," Tim said. "Christian is a very lucky man to have you."

Lisa chuckled. "Well, maybe you should tell him that." She put the last container in the freezer and sighed, satisfied. It was true that helping people really made her feel better. It also helped her get rid of the last remains of that annoying no-good plumber, so, in that sense, she was killing two birds with one stone, now wasn't she?

"There," she said. "It's all in there and ready for you when you need it." She turned to look at Tim again. It hurt her to see him this sad. She grabbed a chair next to him and sat down.

"The worst part is that we ended with a fight, you know?" he said. "I can't bear the fact that I never got to tell her how much I loved her."

"I'm sure she knew."

"How? How could she know? I hardly ever told her. I was too damn proud. If only I had apologized that night. I hate all this guilt."

Lisa nodded pensively. "Why did you have to apologize?"

"It was my fault. It was all my fault that we were fighting the night before," he said and sniffled.

"What was your fault?"

"I should never have told her. I should have kept my big fat mouth shut," he continued.

Lisa put her hand on top of his to comfort him. "I'm sure it doesn't matter anymore. Now you have to focus on your children. They need you, Tim."

"There was this woman," Tim continued, without looking at Lisa.

Lisa froze. She pulled her hand away from his. "What woman?" she asked, slightly anxious for what he was going to tell her. "Tim. What woman?"

"Nothing ever happened. I swear, Lisa. It started at a summer party a couple of months ago. She came on to me."

"Is she an officer?"

"No, one of the assistants. I never told Simone who she was though. She really wanted me to, but I couldn't. She would have killed her."

"Aha. And what exactly happened between you and this assistant?"

"I was in the small kitchen at the station when she came in and started kissing me. I didn't stop her. I know I should have, but I'm ashamed to say I didn't." Tim hid his face in his hands and shook his head. "She kept telling me how badly she wanted me and I... I kissed her back. But nothing else. I swear, Lisa. Nothing else. But ever since that day, she kept coming on to me and grabbing me whenever we were alone, trying to kiss me. It was a nightmare in the end. She kept writing things on Facebook and in emails, and I had no idea how to get it to stop. I told her I wasn't interested, but that didn't make her stop. Then she started calling me in the middle of the night. She kept saying she would tell Simone that I had slept with her if I avoided her. I... I had no idea what to do. So, I told Simone about her. That's why she got so mad at me. She didn't even speak to me all morning... on the day when... the last time I saw her. If I had only apologized and not been so stubborn. I kept telling her that I had no part in it, and she kept arguing that I did because I didn't fight the woman off when she kissed me. Am I such a bad person, Lisa? Am I?"

Lisa snorted, then put her hand on Tim's shoulder. "No, Tim. No, you're not. Tell me again which one of those two assistants at the station was it?"

TWENTY-ONE
NOVEMBER 2013

I worked on my book most of the day. About three o'clock, Sophia popped over with baby Alma in her arms. She looked exhausted.

"What's going on?" I asked when she sat down in my kitchen.

"I can't sleep," she said. "I hardly closed an eye last night."

I shrugged. "Well, you have a baby, that's pretty normal."

She shook her head. Alma played on the floor. "No, not because of her. I'm used to her waking me up; no, I simply can't fall asleep. I keep thinking about Simone. I really liked her. I did, Emma. She was the nicest in our group. I can't believe she's gone. Today someone in my group suggested that her husband could have killed her. Now I can't stop thinking that he might have. Maybe he fooled all of us. I have known my share of psychopaths in my life, and I know how they fool the people around them."

I scoffed. "You know better than to believe stupid rumors and speculations like that. Is there anything that indicates he could have done it?" I asked. "What would his motive have been?"

"Anger, jealousy, because she wanted to leave him. They had a fight. You name it. The man is a police officer, for crying out loud. Those are the worst. Just look at Officer Dan Toft. Remember him?"

"How could I forget?" I mumbled and thought about him for a second. Talk about misjudging people and a true psychopath. "But we can hardly suspect all the police force just because there was one rotten egg."

"True. But still. I'm telling you. Someone shot this woman and he is out there somewhere."

If only it was the husband, I thought and wondered for a second about the missing plumber. *Then at least he wouldn't kill anyone else.*

I stared at Alma who had grabbed on to my chair and was now lifting herself up to stand on two legs. I looked at Sophia.

"She does that all the time now. In a few weeks, she will be walking. Then I'll have to get to work, you know. Constantly chasing her around. When is it again they move away from home?"

"How should I know? Mine are still here," I said, chuckling.

Sophia smiled, then laughed. "They say one day we will sit in our empty houses and look back at this moment and wish for it again. I don't know about that." Sophia laughed again.

"I have a date," I suddenly said.

Sophia lit up. "Really? Whom?"

"Officer Bredballe."

Sophia rolled her eyes. "Finally. That took some time, huh?"

I shrugged. "I don't know. We have been through a lot together."

"When is it?"

"Tomorrow night."

"Oh, we're in a hurry then," Sophia said.

"In a hurry to do what?"

"Get you ready. You need a new dress, we need your hair fixed, and those nails won't do either."

I scoffed. "You must be kidding. Morten isn't into stuff like that."

"Men always say they aren't but they really like it afterward. We'll make you pretty. Come on. Indulge me here. I need this."

"You've got to be kidding me," I said. "I don't have time. I have to write my book, remember?"

"You have plenty of time. You already have two bestsellers, there is no rush with the next one. You have earned plenty of money on the first two."

I frowned. "I really don't want to..."

"Come on. At least go with me to the hairdresser tomorrow morning. The entire mothers' group has planned to go. They have this place where they take care of our babies while they fix our hair. It's new. Please come with me, please? I so badly want to introduce you to my group."

I exhaled deeply. "All right then. But just the hairdresser."

"And a new dress," Sophia said.

"Okay. Hair and dress. But no nails. I can't stand getting my nails done."

"Promise," Sophia said. "Cross my heart and hope to die, stick a needle in my eye."

"Don't say that. I don't like that saying. Why would anyone hope to die? And what's with that needle?"

Sophia rolled her eyes at me again. "All right, Mrs. Cumbersome. I'll just cross my heart then."

"Good."

TWENTY-TWO
NOVEMBER 2013

Susanne's head was hurting badly. The smell was still in her nostrils. She opened her eyes, but saw nothing but darkness. She held a hand to her head, trying hard to remember what had happened. The parking lot. She had been in the parking lot and had just put Malthe in his car seat, yes that was it. Susanne opened her eyes widely.

Malthe? Where is he?

In the darkness, Susanne tried to stand up straight but her head hit against something and she ducked down. Then she fumbled forward across what felt like newspapers on the floor. What was this place?

Susanne tried hard to remember. She had opened the door to her car when someone had approached her. Yes, that was right. Some guy had come up to her. She knew him from somewhere, she had seen him before. Yes, in the café. That was right. He had been in there looking at her and her friends. Where were they now? She had said goodbye to them. Then the guy had come up to her asking her for directions to the post office. He had held a map in his hands. Susanne had thought he was a tourist. She had pointed the direction to him and shown him on the map. He had smiled and nodded. He seemed so nice, she remembered thinking. She wondered why he had been alone and not with some nice family. He looked like a dad, he really did. Except for his eyes. There had been something in them when he had lifted his head and looked at her, thanking her for her help. He had pulled something out of his pocket. What was it?

A cloth, yes, that was it. It had been a white cloth. It had smelled horrible. He had put it over her mouth. Susanne spat on the floor thinking about the horrendous taste it had left her with. She needed something to drink. She was so thirsty. But most of all, she needed to get back to her children.

What if Malthe is still sitting in the car in the parking lot? Oh, my god, he must be so scared. I need to get back. What time is it? I need to pick up Christine. How do I get out of here? Where am I?

"Hello?" she said. "Is there anyone here?"

There was a sound from above. Susanne gasped. It certainly didn't sound human. Susanne reached out and her hand hit something that felt like a net. Her heart dropped.

What was this place? A panic spread quickly in her body. Her hands were shivering. Had that guy brought her here? Had he put her in some kind of cage?

Shivering and panting, Susanne felt her way along the net. It didn't take her long to feel her way around. This was definitely a cage of some sort. She hit the ceiling that was also a wired net of some sort. A loud sound startled her and made her throw herself to the ground with her face on the newspapers.

What was that? It sounded like an animal? Like an animal screaming? Was that? Could it be?

Susanne breathed heavily, trying to lie completely still. Whatever it was that was in there with her, she needed to stay away from it. The animal screamed again. Susanne slowly realized that there was more than one animal, and they weren't staying in one place anymore. They were flying all over the cage.

Bats.

Susanne whimpered when one flew really close to her head. She felt the draft from its wings as it passed her with a high pitched cry. A few seconds after, it happened again, and this time it managed to grab her hair. Susanne screamed as it pulled her hair with its claws and a huge clump was pulled out. She tried to protect herself by hitting into the darkness with her arms, but the bats were too fast. Then she tried yelling and screaming, but the bats were louder. Suddenly, she felt one on her back. She threw herself around trying to knock it off, but it stayed on. Susanne screamed again when it bit her between her shoulder blades. Another bat flew close to her face and Susanne growled and hit her fist into the darkness, but hit the net instead and made a loud sound. Another bite, this time on her shoulder made her scream, then another followed on her leg and yet another on her arm. Susanne was screaming in distress, throwing her body on the ground trying to knock the bats off of her body.

Finally something happened that provided her with a slight hope. The lights were turned on and the bats all screeched before they flew back onto the ceiling, where they grabbed onto the wire with their long claws and covered their small ugly faces with their wings. Susanne gasped and cried. There were so many of them, it almost made her want to throw up. Her back was pounding and the wounds on her arms were bleeding. Susanne was whimpering as the man she remembered from the day before approached her from the other side of the net.

"Please, help me," she pleaded. "Please, let me out of here."

TWENTY-THREE
OCTOBER 2009

The letter came in his mailbox. Thomas suspected it might be bad and waited for hours before he opened it. He stared at it on the table with his heart pounding in his chest and his hands sweaty.

The police had been to his flat twice since the accident in Ellen's garden. Two officers telling him to stay away from the house and from Ellen and her family. On the first visit, they had been nice and talked to him in a harsh, but almost friendly tone. They told him that Ellen and her husband were thankful that Thomas had saved little Gerda, but they wanted him to stay away from now on.

Thomas nodded and told them he would, but when he closed the door he went back to pick up the binoculars and look at Ellen inside the kitchen. She had been cooking lasagna. That was when Thomas knew she didn't mean it. It was his favorite food and she knew that. It was her sign for him, to let him know she didn't want him to stay away; she just had to send the police in order to make her husband happy. Thomas knew the game perfectly well. She still wanted him. She still loved him. All she was telling him was to be more careful from now on.

So Thomas had laid low for a week. He didn't send any flowers and bought no new toys for the children. He still followed Ellen everywhere but made sure not to be seen. After a week, he thought it was enough and sent Ellen the biggest bouquet the shop could provide. He sat in his flat and watched with great joy when she received them.

Two days later the police came to his door again. This time they weren't so friendly. They called him a creep and a pervert and beat him with their batons. Thomas hadn't been able to walk properly for days afterward. But it was okay, he told himself. If this was what he had to go through to be with her, then so be it. His love for Ellen was so profound, he would take any beating any day just to be close to her. It didn't matter. He took what he could get. The small signals letting him know she still loved him were enough to keep him going.

Now he was staring at the letter on the table wondering what it said, but not wanting to find out. He sighed deeply and looked at Ellen who was playing in the garden with Gerda. Then he looked back at the envelope. He picked it up and opened it. His arm was still hurting from the beating.

He read the letter, then put it down on the table again. With his heart pounding heavily in his chest, he watched Ellen push Gerda on the swings.

"You're gonna be late, Ellen," he mumbled while a tear rolled across his cheek. "You have to be at the dentist at two, remember?"

Thomas sighed and watched as Ellen realized they were running late for her appointment. Then he turned and looked at the letter again.

Restraining Order, it said with big black letters on the top. So this was how it was going to be, huh? Well, Thomas wasn't going to let that stupid husband of hers destroy what he had with Ellen. No, he thought he could stop Thomas from seeing and protecting his beloved, but Thomas wasn't going to give up that easily. Ellen needed him and no man or any piece of paper was ever going to keep him away from her.

While the tears rolled across his face, Thomas picked up the letter and looked at it.

To think that he would play a dirty trick like this. Well, if that's the way you want it, then that's what you're getting.

Thomas shredded the letter, then put it in an envelope and wrote Ellen's name and address on the outside of it. He looked at the letter with great satisfaction. This should let her know. This should comfort her and give her the reassurance that Thomas was always going to be there for her. No matter what happened. No husband, no police or court order, was ever going to stop him from protecting her.

No one ever comes between you and me, beloved. No one.

TWENTY-FOUR
NOVEMBER 2013

I didn't want to admit it, but I quite enjoyed being pampered for once. The stylist at the salon cut my hair and put some highlights in. It looked really good once she was done. Sophia didn't enjoy it as much though. One of her friends in the group, a woman named Susanne, hadn't shown up and that worried her senseless. She was walking back and forth in the salon, waiting for it to be her turn.

"Sit down and read a magazine," I said while the stylist finished up my hair. "You're making me nervous wandering around like that, biting your nails."

"I just can't understand where she can be," Sophia said.

"She probably just forgot," another of the women, named Lisa, said. I recognized her picture from one of the posters I had seen on my way to the salon telling me I needed to vote for her in the upcoming election for city council.

"But why doesn't she answer the phone?" Sophia said.

"People are entitled to not answer their phones now and then," I argued. "Just because they have a phone doesn't mean they have to be available at any hour of the day."

"Maybe Malthe had a rough night," Lisa said, with the same

gentle smile that she had on the poster. "Maybe Susanne is simply sleeping, not caring about anything but getting some shut-eye. We all have those kind of days."

"That's exactly what we said about Simone," Sophia said and bit down heavily on a fingernail. "And look at what happened to her!"

Lisa sighed. "We have no idea what happened to Simone or who killed her. Maybe she owed money or something. There is no way for us to know exactly what went on in her life."

"Or it could have been a serial killer who likes to kill mothers with newborn babies," Sophia said.

Lisa burst into laughter. "I have never heard of such a silly thing," she said.

I couldn't help chuckling a little myself. Sophia looked at me like she was hurt. "I'm sorry," I said. "It sounded really funny. Besides you told me yourself that you think the husband did it."

Sophia nodded. Lisa looked at me with a serious face. "Tim? Now that is ridiculous."

Sophia shrugged. She found a chair and sat down. She pulled out her phone and tried to call Susanne once again. When there was no answer, she put the phone down. The babies were being looked after in a room next door. I could hear them babbling happily. Sophia exhaled deeply. "Well. I guess I might be overreacting a little. What do you think, Nora?"

The third woman in the group looked up from her magazine. Sophia had told me about her... that she was always so quiet. She hardly ever spoke a word when the group met, and Sophia felt like she hardly knew her at all. She was the only one in the group who had gone back to work after only six months of maternity leave, instead of staying out the full twelve months that she was entitled to. It was strange, Sophia had thought, while I explained to her that maybe the woman enjoyed her job and really wanted to get back. But Sophia didn't get that. It was difficult for her to see how anyone would give up six months of fully paid leave with their child. I tried to tell her that not everybody enjoyed maternity leave the way she did.

Nora looked at Sophia with startled eyes, like she had never expected any of us to ever address her and now she was afraid of saying something stupid. She had that look like a neglected child, and I wondered if she had a husband who abused her or if she had been abused in her childhood.

"I... I... I really don't know," she said. "Maybe Susanne had something else to do today. Or it could be that killer again." Nora forced an insecure smile, then returned to her magazine looking like she hoped we would leave her alone from now on.

"Well, that was enlightening," Sophia growled. She picked up the phone and called Susanne once again. This time she left a message.

"Hi, Susanne. This is Sophia. We're getting a little worried about you. Well, maybe you just forgot or something, but we are at the salon getting our hair done and afterward, we'll go downtown to look for some new clothes. We'll have lunch at our usual café, if you want to join us later. Anyway, give me a call and let me know you're all right, okay? See ya'."

TWENTY-FIVE
NOVEMBER 2013

He had let her out. Much to her surprise, the strange man had let Susanne get out of the cage and now they were standing in the garage staring at each other. Susanne was wondering what he wanted with her, not daring to ask because the man was pointing his rifle at her. He was grinning from ear to ear while looking at her with menace in his eyes.

This whole ordeal was making Susanne feel scared for the first time in a long time. Usually, nothing ever frightened her. But right now, she was afraid. She was very afraid. Afraid that she was going to die there in that strange garage at the hands of this man, afraid that she was never going to see her children again, frightened for Christine and little Malthe's future without parents. She felt just as scared as she had back when her husband and the father of her two children had been in the hospital bed and the doctors had told her that he wasn't going to make it, that he only had a few days left to live.

They had discovered the tumor the week after Susanne had learned she was pregnant with their second child. It was advanced, the doctor said. And it had spread. He died two weeks before Malthe was born. That was the worst part, Susanne always said... that he never got to see his second child.

"Please, sir. I have children," she said now and looked at the strange man. "They have no father. If you kill me, there is no one to take care of them."

The man tilted his head. The bats were making noises in the cage. A chill went down Susanne's back thinking about how they had been all over her body. Her arm and back were hurting. Did she have a fever? Or was it the anxiety? It was hard to tell.

"I'm sure you have someone to take care of them," the man said. "Grandparents?" He chuckled.

Susanne exhaled. She didn't say anything, but he was right. If she was killed, her mother would take care of Malthe and Christine. No doubt about it. But that was even worse than being orphaned if you asked Susanne. She couldn't do this to her children. She couldn't let them grow up under the same conditions that she had. She had barely gotten out of there with her sanity intact. Susanne felt tears pressing behind her eyes.

"Please, sir. Please, don't do this to me. I beg of you. Let me go. I'll never tell anyone. Have your way with me, rape me if you want to, but please let me see my babies again."

The man stared at her in silence. He seemed to be scrutinizing her, like he was speculating about what she said.

"Please, sir. What do you even want with me? Why me?" she asked.

"Why is not the question. I have my reasons. You have taken something from me and now I'm taking something from you. It's that simple," he said.

Susanne shook her head. "What? What have I ever taken from you? I don't even know you."

"That might be. But I know you."

Susanne stared at the man, feeling helpless. He was clearly as mad as they come. How was she ever going to talk sense into him? Could he be mistaking her for someone else? She couldn't imagine what it was he was talking about.

"Please, sir. I'm sorry if I have done something to you, but I... I have children, for crying out loud. They need me."

"I tell you what," the man said, chewing on a piece of gum. "I'll give you a second chance."

Susanne was startled. What was he saying? Was there hope for her after all? Would she make it out? "I'll do anything you want," she said.

"Good," he said and smiled. Then he leaned over and pushed a button. The wall opened up and a ray of sunlight lit up the room. The garage door opened completely and Susanne gasped when she saw the dirt road that continued into the forest. She looked at the man.

"So what is it you want me to do?" she asked with a pounding heart.

The man grinned, then leaned closer to her face. Susanne gasped in fear.

"I want you to run," he said. "Run as fast as you can."

TWENTY-SIX
NOVEMBER 2013

Lisa couldn't find rest all day. She had spent the morning at the hairdresser's with her group. All of them had annoyed her immensely, even that extra woman who the loud-talking Sophia had brought along with her. Lisa knew who she was. She was that author who had written two bestselling books about horrendous things happening on Fanoe island years ago or something. Lisa hadn't had the time to read them and probably never would, but it was bad to be seen in that woman's company. She wasn't very popular right now among the people on the island, even if her books had made Fanoe a popular tourist attraction among the rest of the population. Lisa was upset with Sophia for having brought that woman along and making Lisa look bad in the eyes of her possible voters. It was just so typical of Sophia to never think about anyone but herself.

Lisa hit her fist into the steering wheel in anger and wondered if she should drive past Sophia's and teach her a lesson once and for all. No, there was no time for that now. There was someone else who annoyed her even more. Lisa had been thinking about her all day, not being able to get her out of her head again. Not after what Tim had told her about this woman. How could anyone be so idiotic and selfish as to come on to a married man? And she was even married herself. It was simply not something nice people did. She should have known better.

Appalling. Inexcusable. Horrendous.

Margrethe was fussing in the back seat while Lisa drove into her driveway. She parked in the garage and took her baby out. She put her in the playpen while thinking about this woman and how somebody ought to teach her a lesson.

Lisa clapped her hands in joy. Oh, how she would love to be the one to do it. She went into the kitchen and started baking biscuits for her family. As she put them in the oven, the telephone rang. She picked it up.

"Yes?"

"Lisa Rasmussen?"

"Yes. Who is this?"

"Per Egon."

Lisa froze.

"Do you know who I am?" he asked.

"I think I do."

"Great, then you also know that you don't stand a chance against me, right? I have had my eye on that seat on the city council that you want for eight years and I'm going to get it," he said. "You might as well pull out right now."

Lisa laughed. It was true that yesterday someone had pulled out of the race for city council and now there was one seat open. An elderly member had announced that he was retiring. Lisa knew there were two who wanted it, because the rest of the seats were spoken for. Per Egon was a local hero, born and raised on the island, the son of a former very popular mayor, whereas Lisa had just moved to the island. She had the odds against her, but that had never been an obstacle before in her life. Lisa was going to win this no matter what it took.

"Well, if you're so sure, then why do you feel the need to call me and tell me all this?"

Per Egon went quiet. "I'm just trying to save you from being publicly humiliated. But if that is what you want, Lisa Rasmussen, then by all means, be my guest. But I tell you there is no chance in hell you'll ever get that seat."

"I wouldn't be so sure if I were you," Lisa said, staying calm and fighting every urge to yell at the man.

"Oh, but I am."

Lisa forced a loud laugh. "Well, I guess the fight is on then."

"Oh, it is on."

Then he hung up. Lisa threw her phone on the table. The back of it fell off.

Bastard. Prick. Who the hell does he think he is? Doesn't he know who I am? I'll show him and this whole damn town.

Lisa picked up her phone and put the back on. Then she turned it on. It still worked. The biscuits were done just as Amalie came through the door. Lisa put on her best and most gracious smile. Amalie looked at her mother with the biscuits in front of her, then she rolled her eyes.

"Don't you know how many calories there are in those?" She scoffed and ran upstairs.

Lisa felt the anger rise, but kept it inside with a forced smile. Like so many days before this, Lisa swallowed her rage and smiled. She kept smiling the rest of the evening when Christian came home with Jacob and all the way through dinner. She even smiled when her husband told her that she was being stupid for spending all this time and his money on this foolish election and then took off to go to the bar and hang out with his friends, while she had to put the kids to bed by herself.

But when midnight came and she snuck out of bed, she smiled no more.

TWENTY-SEVEN
NOVEMBER 2013

"You look lovely."

Officer Morten Bredballe smiled when I opened the door. I blushed. "Do you like the hair? I had it done this morning."

"You look stunning," he said. "But you always do."

"Aw, that's such a nice thing to say," I said and grabbed my jacket. "I'm leaving now, Maya," I yelled.

"Okay," she yelled back.

I shrugged. "That's about the most she speaks to me these days," I said with a smile and closed the door behind me.

"Sounds familiar," Morten said as we started walking. "Jytte hardly ever utters an entire sentence to me anymore. It's mostly grunting and mumbling. But I'll take what I can get, you know?"

I laughed. The icy wind bit my cheeks on our way to his car. It was getting really cold now. I drew in a deep breath when he opened the door and held it for me. I liked the fresh air here on the island. It was really different from in the city. Colder and definitely more windy, yes, but it had this rawness and freshness to it that I had never experienced before. I enjoyed it a lot even when it got colder. I felt healthier and stronger here. And I felt like my kids were too. I was still very happy to have moved here even with all the bad things that had been going on. I had a feeling things were going to shape up soon. I looked at Morten when we were in the car. He wasn't a handsome man, but he had such nice eyes and the best smile. I loved making him smile and laugh. One thing I had learned on our trips to Eastern Europe was that he had a great sense of humor. I enjoyed that a lot, as in my marriage to Michael we never laughed at any of the same things. Actually Michael hardly ever laughed. He was so serious all the time and never understood my jokes or even pretended to. He thought I was foolish and scolded me for not taking anything serious. In his eyes, I couldn't do anything right.

Morten took me to a small downtown restaurant named La Petite Cuisine. He told me it was his favorite place. The food was great, even if I had had better, but the company was exquisite. Morten was so sweet and caring, and he laughed at every joke I made. Not because he wanted to impress me or anything, but he really laughed with all his heart because he thought it was funny. It felt good to just forget about everything else for a few hours. He seemed a little shy and hardly shared anything about himself, and I did most of the talking, but I didn't mind. He seemed genuinely interested in what I had to say.

"Did the plumber ever show up?" I asked when the dessert arrived.

Morten shook his head. "Not yet. He might have taken the ferry to the mainland to drink. I hope he'll turn up when he runs out of money. He hasn't been using any of his credit cards though, which is odd. We have asked the bank to alert us when they see he is using one of them."

I nodded and ate a scoop of my vanilla ice cream with hot cherry sauce. "Sounds strange if he is on a bender."

Morten shrugged. "He might be using cash."

"True," I said pensively. "What about Simone Beaumont?"

"What about her?"

"Anything new in the investigation?" I asked. "I can't help wondering about the car. Did she drive it into the ocean on her own or what?"

Morten shook his head. "She was dead before it hit the water. Hours before, according to the forensic report."

I lifted an eyebrow. "Then who drove the car?"

"Whoever shot her must have placed her behind the wheel, then turned the car on and put the car in gear with the intention of having her drive into the ocean. Maybe he thought we wouldn't find her in there or something."

"Hardly a very good hiding spot," I said with my mouth full of ice cream. "Whom did the car belong to?"

"It was a stolen Land Rover. The owners told us it was stolen a couple of weeks ago. It was taken from outside their house in Vejle."

"That's on the mainland."

"I know."

"So the killer is not from around here, you think?" I asked.

Morten shrugged again. "Well, it's hard to say, but my theory is that he is from the mainland. That he came here and killed Simone, maybe for no specific reason at all, then got rid of the body and the stolen car before he left the island, maybe even on foot. You know, just by taking the ferry back."

"So you think he is gone?"

Morten exhaled. "I sincerely hope he is." He rubbed his face, then looked at me with a smile. He grabbed my hand across the table. "Let's talk about something nice. I hate talking about work."

I chuckled. "You're so right. I'm sorry. I was just being curious. So Jytte is in high school. What does she want to do when she is done?"

Morten laughed. "You're really bad at this," he said.

"I know. I'm sorry."

He held my hand in his and looked at my fingers. I tried hard to find something to say that wasn't related to his work. "So tell me about your ex-wife, Jytte's mom. Where is she?"

Morten let go of my hand and leaned back with a deep sigh. "I was hoping to avoid that question for a little while longer," he said.

"Okay," I said. "Whenever you're ready to tell."

"Thanks," he said. "I might need a little time."

"That's okay."

"Good."

Naturally, that was all I was wondering about the rest of the evening. All I knew was that Morten was alone with Jytte. I had no idea if the mother was still in his life in any way and now I feared that she was. I was afraid he was still helplessly in love with her or something. It left me feeling stirred up inside that he wouldn't tell me about her.

"You're so quiet all of a sudden," he said in the car on our way home.

I forced a smile. "I'm just tired, that's all."

And I'm wondering if you're still secretly in love with your ex, that's all, I thought but never said it out loud, naturally.

He parked the car in front of my house and escorted me to the door. My heart was pounding in my chest. Should I invite him in for coffee? Do I want to? I realized I didn't. I felt insecure and kept picturing this ex-wife of his as this gorgeous, perfect woman whom he dreamed about at night. Then I wondered if he was going to say her name during the act if I ever let him into my bed.

"I would invite you in, but... I have a busy day tomorrow, so..." I said.

Morten looked disappointed. "That's okay. I'll just..." he leaned over and kissed me awkwardly on the cheek. "I have an early shift too," he said.

"Plus Victor hasn't been sleeping well lately, so..." I kept excusing myself.

"No, no, that's okay. Victor is important. He needs his sleep, right? Maybe... So maybe I can call you or... ?"

"Yeah. Sure. Call me sometime." I exhaled and looked at him. "I'm sorry," I said.

"No, no. You don't have to be. I understand. I'll see you around." Morten started walking. I bit my tongue. This evening had been so nice up until that awkward moment that ruined everything.

Say something nice. Something that'll make him feel better. Say something before he leaves and it ends like this. You like him, for Pete's sake.

I closed my eyes and opened my mouth to speak.

"I..."

Morten turned around and interrupted me. "I'm sorry," he said. "Could we please start over? I had a great night. I would really like to see you again."

"I'm sorry too," I said. "I'm being silly here."

"No, you're being reasonable. It's better to take things slowly. I am just really... really attracted to you."

I blushed like a schoolgirl and had no words.

"But you're so right," he continued. "It is much better to wait. Plus there is the whole ex-wife thing. I noticed how it bothered you, and I could have bit my tongue off afterward. It's just that it was really a bad time for me, and I didn't want to ruin a great evening by telling my sad sob story."

I felt stupid. I walked closer, then leaned over and kissed him on the lips. I closed my eyes while kissing him.

"Wow," he said afterward.

"Let's do this again soon," I said.

"Let's."

Smiling, I turned and walked back toward the house.

Morten was still staring at me as I opened the front door. I turned and looked at him one last time.

"Good night," I said.

"Good night," he replied, then waved and walked back to his car.

I grabbed another glass of red wine before bed and sat outside on the porch looking at my back garden while drinking it. I didn't feel tired yet, so I decided to take a stroll through the garden down to the beach. It was cold, but the night was clear and starry and I loved these quiet nights. I walked for a long time across the sand dunes thinking about my life and the men in it. I really liked Morten but didn't dare fall head over heels for him. I had been burned too much to do so. People always came with baggage and I still hadn't been allowed to look into his. I remembered being completely taken with my ex, Michael, and how I had been so blind with love that I didn't see the warning signals. I remembered my dad talking to me about it before we were married. He tried to warn me, telling me that Michael had a coldness to him that he didn't care for. He told me that a thing like that was only going to get worse the older Michael got and that I should be aware of it when making my decision. But his warning only made me want to marry Michael even more.

I scoffed and stopped at the top of a dune. I listened to the sound of the raging ocean. Why was it that I hadn't listened to him? It would have spared me so much sorrow in my life. But done was done and if I had never married Michael I would never have had Victor or Maya, and there was no way I wanted a life without them.

I took in a deep breath of the fresh air and thought about Jack. I had really liked him too, and I knew he liked me a lot, but it was just so complicated. Up until tonight Morten hadn't seemed complicated at all. But of course he had his baggage as well. Everyone had something, didn't they?

I started walking again. I had been doing this a lot lately, taking long walks on the beach in the evenings before bed. The fresh air had a way of knocking me out afterward, and I slept so well. I realized I had walked too far and was about to turn around when a sound made me look. From the top of a dune, I spotted a car that entered the beach and drove across the sand toward the ocean at a high speed. I felt frozen and had no idea what to do. Motionless, I stared at the car as it drove straight into the ocean and kept going till it was covered with water.

Then I ran. While calling Morten from my phone, I ran as fast as I could.

TWENTY-EIGHT
NOVEMBER 2013

I threw my phone on the sand with my jacket and jumped into the water. The ice-cold water felt like knives against my body, but I didn't care. I swam as fast as I could toward where the car had gone in. Waves tossed me around and pushed me back toward the beach. I ducked and tried to swim under them, then came up for air and was smashed in the face by a wave. I swallowed water and coughed. Then I ducked under again. I couldn't see anything, and I had to get up for more air. The water was so cold; I was freezing while I frantically scanned the area to spot the car, but I saw nothing. I dived into the ocean again and somehow bumped into something that I guessed was it. I came up for more air, then dove down toward it, feeling my way across the roof and down toward the door. I tried to pull it open, but it was stuck. I swam to the surface again and gasped for air. A light hit me from the beach. Between waves, I spotted cars on the beach. The bright lights helped me see. I dove down once again and managed to pull the door open and grab the body inside of it. I pulled it out and toward the surface. I gasped and tried to yell for help. The heavy body was difficult for me to hold on to.

"HELP!" I yelled.

A wave tossed over me and I swallowed more water. I tried to swim toward the shore on my back dragging the body after me, but I was so tired now, it was hard. I pulled and fought the waves that kept washing over my face.

Come on, Emma. Just a little more. Come on. You can do it. Fight for it. Don't give up.

A wave flushed in over my head, and I coughed to breathe. I was tumbled and lost my grip on the body. I tried to scream but couldn't. Suddenly I felt hands on my body, and I was pulled toward the beach.

"The body," I gasped when I was out of the water. I opened my eyes and looked into Morten's. He was dripping on me from his hair and clothes.

"We've got her," he said, panting. "The paramedics are taking care of her."

I coughed up water on the sand. "Is she alive?" I said.

Morten looked in the direction of the ambulance and the paramedics. "I have no idea. It looks like they're trying to revive her, so maybe she is. What about you? Are you all right?"

I coughed again. "I will be," I said.

One of the paramedics ran to me and kneeled beside me. He put a thick blanket around my back to warm me.

"I'm okay," I said.

"I need to make sure," the paramedic said.

"I'm fine. Take care of the woman instead."

"Okay," he said and left me.

I sat up and stared at Morten. He was catching his breath. His lips were purple and shivering. "We should get out of here," I said. "We need to get out of these wet clothes."

Morten stared around us. Officers were blocking the entrance to the beach with cars and keeping curious spectators back.

Morten got up and grabbed my hand to pull me up as well. "I'll take you home," he said.

He helped me get inside my house. I couldn't hold my keys and unlock the door because my fingers were hurting. My teeth chattered now, and my nails had turned purple.

"You were really brave... and a little stupid tonight," Morten said while helping me get up the stairs.

I tried to laugh but couldn't. Morten opened the door to the bathroom, then helped me get inside. He turned on the hot water tap and started filling the tub.

"This should get your blood circulation up and running in no time," he said.

I nodded and tried to say something but my lips quivered too much. Morten looked at me, then took off the blanket. He started undressing me. I could hardly move. He took off all of my clothes one by one, then looked at me with a smile.

"This wasn't exactly how I pictured myself seeing you naked the first time," he said, and helped me into the warm water. It hurt so badly when the water hit my frozen body parts.

Morten was shivering all over too and got undressed. Then he got into the tub with me. He grabbed my body and held his close to mine to warm me up. It felt really nice.

We stayed in there for almost all night. When I was finally able to speak properly again, I looked up at him with a small smile.

"This has to be the strangest first date I have ever been on."

"It's definitely made my top ten as well," he said.

Then we both laughed. It felt good to laugh.

TWENTY-NINE
NOVEMBER 2013

Nora Willumsen had trouble sleeping. It wasn't the baby who kept her awake, at least not tonight. And it wasn't her husband Erik who was snoring next to her either. No, it was the thought of Tim being all alone at his house now that his wife was gone. Yes, it was sad and horrible what happened to her, but to be honest Nora had never liked the bitch, and she couldn't have planned it better, now could she? Now Tim was alone, abandoned, lonely, and that was when she would sweep in and make him fall madly in love with her.

Nora had tried to get his attention for years. But it wasn't until the summer party a few months ago that she had succeeded. She had kissed him in the kitchen at the police station where they had worked together, and she had secretly admired him for years.

Nora had been the only one in her mothers' group to go back to work before her maternity leave was up, and she knew how the others looked at her. She was only able to participate in the group meetings and activities on her days off, but she didn't care. Staying home for six months without seeing Tim was unbearable. Hanging out almost every day with his wife was just pure torture. How many times had Nora dreamed about killing Simone herself? Just picking up the steak knife from the table at the café and stabbing the woman in the chest, finishing her off so she could finally be the only one in Tim's life.

Nora chuckled in her bed and put a hand over her mouth so Erik wouldn't hear her. Now that Simone was really gone, she would have to find a way to get rid of Erik too. He was nothing but an obstacle in her life now. The only one between her and Tim.

Nora couldn't lie still. She was tossing and turning thinking about Tim and how wonderful everything was going to be as soon as he realized how much he loved her. Erik grunted in his sleep and Nora froze. The last thing she wanted right now was to wake him up. She wouldn't want to risk him touching her or in any way wanting to kiss her. She had tried hard to avoid it lately and especially she had avoided having sex with him. Oh, the horror if she ever had to do that again. She loathed his big hands and his ugly beard that always hurt her when he kissed her. She loathed every line in his face and the fact that he was getting fatter and fatter every day now. No, she had to find a way to get rid of him. She had thought about just leaving him, but he would never let her go. He had told her that on numerous occasions.

"I'll kill you if you ever leave me," he always said.

Nora took off the covers and walked to the bathroom where she looked at herself in the mirror. The bruises on her stomach and back were better. It had been at least a week since he last beat her up. She had gotten better at avoiding his anger and pleasing him. Now, she wondered if she might be able to poison him and get away with it. Just slip it in his evening drink. She could use rat poisoning. They had a lot of it in the basement; Erik used the poison for work as an exterminator. Oh, how she even loathed what he did for a living. Everything about him was just so... so disgusting and sickening. He was repulsive.

Nora sighed, then walked to the bedroom next door where her little Maria slept in her crib. Erik hadn't touched her yet, and he was never going to. Nora was going to make sure of that. She put the baby's blanket over her small body, then walked out. In the hallway, she was startled by a strange sound coming from downstairs. What was that? Was someone in the kitchen?

Probably just Erik getting a midnight snack. If he keeps stuffing his face like this I won't have to kill him. He'll do that on his own.

Nora sighed and wanted to go back to bed, but something made her stop. It was the sound of the timer on the oven.

Erik never cooks. He doesn't even know how to turn on the oven. Why would he set the timer?

Nora closed her bathrobe, then walked closer to the end of the stairs and looked down. The light was on and someone was definitely down there. What was that? Was that someone humming?

Nora walked down the stairs and into the kitchen. She gasped, startled at the sight that met her there.

"Lisa?"

Lisa turned to look at her. On the cooker, Nora's big pot was boiling. Lisa was holding a handful of scallions in her hand.

"Oh, hi, Nora. Did I wake you up?"

Nora shook her head. What was this? She could hardly believe it. This had to be the strangest thing she had ever seen. "Lisa? What... What the hell are you doing in my kitchen?"

Lisa grabbed the big knife, swung it through the air with a smile and chopped the scallions really fast, like a chef in a restaurant. Then she placed all of them inside the boiling pot.

"Isn't it obvious?" Lisa asked.

"Isn't what obvious?"

"Stew. I'm making a stew."

"What are you talking about, Lisa? It's in the middle of the night. What are you doing in my house? Cooking? Have you completely lost it? I always suspected you were off, but this?"

Lisa tilted her head like she was speculating about what Nora had said. "It's funny how it's always the quiet ones who cause the most trouble, isn't it?"

"What?" Nora sighed. "Just get out of here, will you?"

"It's funny how you had all of us fooled with your little quiet act, isn't it?" Lisa picked up a bundle of carrots and started chopping them.

"I really don't..." Nora said.

Lisa turned to face her and pointed the knife toward her. Nora gasped. Lisa looked like a madwoman. "Don't you know that what you did was very WRONG?"

"What are you talking about?" Nora said and backed away from her. At least far enough to be out of reach.

Lisa walked slowly closer. "You kissed him, Nora. You kissed someone else's husband, knowing he was married and just had his second child. That is WRONG, Nora. There is one important rule you never break in life. You never EVER go after someone else's husband. That is OFF limits." When Lisa spoke the last words, she lifted the knife and stabbed it through Nora's hand that was resting on the counter. Nora screamed. Lisa placed her hand over her mouth. "Now, don't wake up that sweet little husband of yours, all right. I don't think you'd want him to know what I know, do you?"

Nora whimpered in pain behind the gloved hand pressed against her lips. Then she shook her head.

"Good," Lisa said. She removed the hand from Nora's mouth, then returned to her cooking. She pulled out another knife from the knife block and continued chopping the carrots.

Nora stared at her hand that was nailed to the wooden counter. Tears rolled across her cheeks. Blood was dripping onto the white floor underneath. She couldn't move. She tried to grab the handle of the knife and pull it out, but it was too painful.

"Now," Lisa said and poured the carrots inside the pot. "All we need is some spices and..." she turned to look at Nora. She stroked her gently across her cheek. Nora tried to move, but it hurt too badly.

Lisa smiled maniacally. "And, of course... the most important ingredient." Lisa stared at Nora with piercing eyes. "The meat."

THIRTY

JANUARY 2013

They were packing up. Thomas watched them through the binoculars with a pounding heart. Ellen was in the kitchen putting things into boxes, wrapping the plates nicely so they wouldn't break while being transported. The handsome husband was carrying the chairs from the dining room into a big lorry parked outside. Three big men were helping him. It had all gone really fast. Thomas had woken up the same morning to the sound of the lorry arriving and it didn't take him long to realize what was going on. Frantically, he had been watching them for hours, and now they were almost done.

How come he hadn't seen this coming? How come she hadn't told him about this? Not a signal, not a sign, not a word had he heard from her. She had to be scared, he soon concluded. The husband probably forced her to move.

Thomas growled while watching the husband carry out a heavy table with one of the moving guys. Thomas imagined the table falling on the husband and killing him. Oh, what a joy it would be if the man would just die right here and now. Or vanish somehow. He was the only obstacle between Thomas and Ellen. Always had been.

Thomas found his phone and called Ellen's number. He looked at her while waiting for her to pick up. If he gave her the chance, she could manage to tell him where they were going once she picked up. Finally it went through, but Ellen wasn't moving in the kitchen, she wasn't picking up the phone. A cold and indifferent voice on the other end spoke: "This number is no longer in service."

Thomas threw the phone across the room in anger. He clenched both his fists while staring at Ellen through the window.

"Where are you going, Ellen?" he said to the room. He stormed to the window once again. The lorry was still there, but they were almost done packing it. How long had she known about this? A move like that took planning, didn't it? She could at least have hinted to him, so he could start preparing as well. She had to leave him a clue somehow, she simply had to. She loved him too much to be able to leave him like this. They couldn't live without each other. It would kill the both of them.

Damn that husband! It is all his fault. He is forcing her to do this. He is forcing her to leave me. I'll kill him. I'm going to fucking kill that bastard!

The moving men closed the back of the lorry and the movers sat in the front seat. They said something to the handsome husband then drove off. Ellen and her family got into another car.

"They're leaving. Hurry up," Thomas shrieked and grabbed his coat and ran outside and jumped down the stairs taking several steps at a time.

If you follow them, they'll show you where they're going. She wants you to follow them. That's what she wants.

Thomas stormed out the door and toward his car, still with his eyes fixated on Ellen's car. She was holding the door for Gerda to get in.

They're still here. You have time. Just get behind the wheel and follow them. Don't let them out of sight and you'll be fine.

Thomas walked toward his car, still staring at Ellen waiting for her to look at him, waiting for her signal that she wanted him to do this, wanted him to follow her. And just like that, it happened. Right before she opened the door to the car's passenger seat, she turned her head and looked directly at him. Then she nodded. It was a nod he couldn't misunderstand. Thomas smiled widely and nodded back. He watched her as she got inside the car, then turned and sprang for his own.

But he never made it that far. Two officers jumped out of a parked car next to his and approached him showing their badges.

"Going somewhere, Thomas?" one of them asked.

The other shook his head. "I think you're staying here for a little while." Then he lifted his baton and swung it through the air hitting Thomas in the neck, knocking him out instantly.

THIRTY-ONE
NOVEMBER 2013

Lisa felt such a thrill as she beat up Nora. She breathed in a deep breath, then lifted her clenched fist and slammed it into her face again and again. A tooth flew out and blood ran down her chin from her split lip. Nora had lost consciousness a little too early, Lisa thought. She had made the mistake of slamming the thick wooden cutting board in her face to begin with and after that Nora had barely been awake enough for it to be really fun.

But this will have to do, Lisa thought and slammed her clenched fist into Nora's face once again.

Lisa was sweating from all the excitement and wiped her face on her sleeve. She was too smart to use one of Nora's towels and leave DNA behind. No, Lisa was so much smarter than that. The only thing she was afraid of now was that Nora's husband would wake up and come downstairs. If he did, she would have to deal with him as well. There was still room in the freezer at home. But apparently Erik was a heavy sleeper as, so far, he had slept through all the turmoil and Nora occasionally waking up screaming before she lost consciousness completely.

Lisa hit her one final time, then pulled out the knife that

had gone through Nora's hand. It made a delicious sound as it came loose. Lisa shivered in delight. The hand fell to the ground next to the nearly lifeless Nora.

Lisa kneeled next to her and listened. She was still breathing, but not for long. Lisa panted, then walked to grab the butcher knife. She bent over Nora and started planning what she was going to cut off first.

"The fingers are the easiest part," she mumbled. "But they won't do as meat. The best meat is on the stomach and thighs. With those fat thighs, she'll make a great stew. The rest I'll have to put in the grinder for later use. I'm thinking sausages, lots of them."

Lisa giggled thinking about all the times Christian had applauded her food lately, not knowing what he was eating. For a second, she wondered if it was possible to make a smoothie of meat? She had never tried, but maybe it was about time she did. Lots of good protein in that.

Lisa looked at Nora and stroked her bloody cheeks. "Sorry, but it ends here, little Nora. If only you had made better choices, then this wouldn't be necessary." Lisa was about to start cutting the meat off of Nora's right thigh, when suddenly someone was at the back door. Lisa froze and lifted her eyes to look. A shadow was moving outside the door. She saw it through the frosted door window. Lisa gasped. It couldn't be Erik, could it? He was upstairs sleeping, wasn't he?

The handle turned downward and someone was fiddling with the lock when they realized it was already unlocked, just like Lisa had realized a couple of hours earlier. The door slowly opened and Lisa hid in the pantry next to her. She held her breath and looked out through the crack. A man entered through the door and closed it after him. Then he walked toward Nora and kneeled next to her. Lisa sized him up and decided she could easily take him out. Probably nothing but a burglar picking the wrong house at the wrong time, she thought, and felt the weight of the butcher knife in her hand. The man studied Nora's face, then bent over to listen to see if there was a pulse.

Lisa snorted, then clenched the knife in her hand and prepared herself for her upcoming attack. She put her hand on the door, took in a deep breath, and thought it through. She was going to storm out, then stab the man in the back, hopefully killing him instantaneously; if not, then she'd have to pull it out and stab him again. The man was big, but he was no match for Lisa. She exhaled, grabbed the door to the pantry, but then something happened that made her stop.

The burglar bent down, grabbed Nora's arm, and pulled her onto his back. Lisa stared, startled, as he carried her toward the door, opened it and left with Nora on his back.

Baffled, Lisa stayed in the pantry for a long time before she finally decided she should probably leave as well.

THIRTY-TWO
NOVEMBER 2013

Morten stayed at my house all night. After the bath, we went to my bedroom and, still shaking, we snuggled up together under the covers and fell asleep. When I woke up the next morning, I felt much better. Morten was still sleeping. I turned and looked at him. He was smiling in his sleep. I leaned over and kissed his forehead, then crawled out of the bed and got dressed. I went downstairs to start breakfast. It was Saturday, but Maya had dance class and Victor was always up early, especially on the weekends when he finally got to play outside all day.

He was sitting at the kitchen table when I came in. "Victor. You startled me," I said. I looked at him. He sat bent over his notebook, while writing in it. "How long have you been up?"

Victor stopped writing and looked up. His eyes met mine and I smiled. His eyes were always so serious. It was like he was carrying so much worry inside of him, when all I wanted for him was to be a child, play, and have fun. I never knew what went on inside of that small head of his and I worried constantly about him. Because he never spoke much, I never knew how he was feeling... If he was sad or as troubled as he seemed. With Maya, it was always so different. She had told me every little emotion she ever had all of her life to the extent that I, at one point, stopped taking them seriously because there was always something. Now she had closed up as well, but that was normal behavior for a teenager. With Victor, nothing was normal. I hadn't talked to any of his doctors about him since we had moved away from the city. I was tired of them constantly telling me he was sick and wanting to medicate him. Yes, Victor was introvert and not like other kids, but I could handle him.

"The bats again, huh?" I asked.

Victor nodded.

"Do you hear them now?"

Victor stared at me. Then he nodded. "They'll be quiet soon. When the sun rises," he said. "Then they usually fall asleep. Except when someone is in the cage with them. The smell of blood wakes them up."

I looked at Victor. His eyes were still so serious. I had no idea what to say. I nodded and went to open the freezer. I pulled out some bread and turned on the oven.

"Will Morten have breakfast with us?" Victor asked.

I turned and looked at him. "How did you know he was here?"

Victor shrugged. He looked down at his notebook then continued writing. I made scrambled eggs, soft-boiled eggs, and fried eggs, then heated the bread in the oven and cut it up for Victor.

"Put the book away while you eat," I said and put a plate with his buttered bread and scrambled eggs on the table in front of him.

Victor closed the book and pushed it aside. I poured him some orange juice and put it on the table. He picked it up and drank. I took a chair next to him and sat on it. I tried to catch his eye and have him look at me again, but without luck.

"You're okay, aren't you, Victor? Do you feel sad on the inside? Do you worry about some stuff we should talk about?"

Victor didn't answer. He ate his food without looking at me. I guess he didn't think my questions were important enough to answer.

"Do you miss your father? I can understand if you do."

Still no reaction. Victor ate and drank like he couldn't care less about me or what I was saying. I chuckled, feeling silly.

"Of course you're all right. I'm just being obsessive, right?" I said and got up from the chair. I walked to the cooker and removed the boiling pot of eggs.

"Smells good," a voice said from the door.

I turned and smiled. "You're up."

Morten smiled and nodded at Victor. "Hi, buddy. Do you mind if I take a seat next to you?"

Victor didn't answer. "Don't mind him," I said. "Sit wherever you like."

Morten smiled and sat down. I served him some bread and eggs, then sat next to him with my own plate and started eating. It was very quiet at the table for a long time, and I started feeling awkward.

"Are you on duty today?" I asked to make conversation.

"Yep," Morten said and looked at the clock. "Have to be at the station at ten. Gonna be another busy day, I guess, with all that went down last night."

"Are the people from Copenhagen still in town to help you out with the case?" I asked.

"Yes. Now that we've had a second case, I'm sure they'll stay for a lot longer. It's good. With Tim out of the picture, we are kind of short on men."

"I bet."

Victor emptied his glass of juice and pushed his plate to the middle of the table the way he always did when he was done with his food. Without even looking at me or Morten, he got up from his seat. He grabbed his notebook and stood with it in his hands for a little while, his head bent and his hair falling into his face so we couldn't see his eyes.

"What's wrong, Victor?" I asked. "Is there something you want?"

Victor didn't move or speak.

"Victor? Did you want to say something to Morten?"

Victor finally moved. He took two steps toward Morten, then reached out the notebook toward him.

Morten looked at me, confused.

"Victor?" I asked. I was confused as well. Usually Victor kept that notebook close to himself and he hardly even let me look at it. "Victor? What is it, buddy?"

Victor didn't speak, he just stood with the notebook between his hands pointing it toward Morten.

"I think... Do you think he wants me to take it?" Morten asked.

I shrugged, slightly baffled. "I have no idea. Usually, he never lets any of us look in it, but maybe he likes you. I don't know."

"Should I take it? I don't want to do something wrong."

"With Victor, it's hard to know what is right and wrong," I said.

Victor took a step closer still with the book pointing toward Morten. Now it was touching his arm.

"I think he wants me to take the book," Morten said.

I inhaled deeply. "Is that what you want, Victor?" When he didn't answer I looked at Morten. "I think you're right. Just take it."

"Okay," Morten said and grabbed the book. As he put his hands on it, Victor let go and stormed out the room without a word. Morten looked at me.

"Was it wrong?"

I chuckled. "No. If it was wrong he would have screamed. Storming out the room is when Victor is happy. Probably going into the garden to play." I sipped my coffee and smiled at Morten. "He must like you. That's a good sign."

"But what do I do with it?"

"You read it. He wouldn't have given it to you if he didn't want you to read it," I said.

Morten chuckled, then put the book carefully on the table. He opened the front and started flipping through the pages.

"Makes no sense, right?" I asked and took another piece of bread from the basket. I buttered it and put jam on it while Morten kept flipping the pages. I realized he seemed to be interested in what he was reading.

"Actually, it makes perfect sense to me," Morten said.

I almost choked on my bread. "It does? How so?"

"It might be hard to believe, but before I was a cop, I was a scientist. A biologist and expert on animal echolocation."

"Really?"

"Yes. I worked at Aalborg University. We observed bats and..."

"Bats?"

"Yes, you know how they use echolocation to find insects or animals, even when it's dark? That's what we tried to identify and survey with the hope of being able to help blind people use this technique."

"So what you're saying is that what Victor has written in his notebook has something to do with bats and echolocation?" I asked, startled as I stared at the many numbers and charts.

"This looks exactly like my work, except it seems to be much more accurate. I can't believe your son wrote this."

Morten looked at me like I was trying to trick him or something.

I put my hands in the air. "I have no idea what it is. To me it is nothing but letters and numbers."

Morten shook his head in disbelief. "I don't understand this. How?" he looked at me for an explanation.

I shrugged. "I have no idea."

"How could he have done this?" Morten asked. "How would he know how to depict the sounds? Did he draw this? These charts and numbers show the bats' vocalizations. How can he hear them? Bat calls are in a frequency mostly beyond the range of the human ear."

I was about to drink from my cup, but put it down to not drop it. "Are you telling me he heard this?" I asked.

Morten shook his head. He flipped more pages and stared at them. "I have no idea what I'm saying. It's impossible. Yet I have never seen anything like this. But how would he write these things without the proper instruments? Some of the sounds bats make, we can hear, but not the ones he depicts here on these charts..." Morten paused. He looked at me again.

"I had no idea. I thought it was just random numbers. He hardly ever lets me look at it."

Morten nodded. Then he smiled. "You know what?"

"What?"

There is no way that kid could know these things that people go to university for years to learn. I think he must have copied it from somewhere. Maybe he just picked it up from the internet or something and then copied it in his book. That has to be the explanation. Yes, that is probably it."

I sipped my coffee pensively while nodding but not agreeing. I knew my Victor too well. He heard them all right. That was why they kept him awake at night. And by giving the notebook to Morten, he was trying to tell us something.

THIRTY-THREE
FEBRUARY 2013

Thomas hadn't slept in days. Only an hour here and there on the couch. The rest of the days and nights he used to try to locate Ellen. After he had been knocked out by the police officers on the day Ellen moved away, they had thrown him in prison and kept him for twenty-four hours. When they let him go, he could hardly walk and had to spend three days in bed to recover from his bruising.

They had told him they were keeping an eye on him and that he should stay away from Ellen and, if he tried to find her, they would beat him up again.

But Thomas didn't care. They could beat him all they wanted to. He wasn't going to give up on his great love. Life was simply not worth living without her. At first, he had tried to locate her via Facebook. That used to work, but now her account had been closed, and he couldn't find a new one under her name or anything similar. Thomas figured the husband and the police were behind all of this. They were the ones keeping Ellen away from him, and it hurt him so badly to know that she was somewhere out there all alone with no one to protect her from that husband of hers. It tormented Thomas that the husband could do with her as he pleased from now on. Day and night, he kept imagining all the bad things that husband of hers would do to her.

When Thomas recovered, he went to her house and broke into it going in through the small window in the basement, like he used to. First he went through the bedroom upstairs, but it was completely empty. It saddened him deeply to see this vacant room that reminded him that he had lost his beloved.

In the kitchen, he found an old rubbish bag that they had left behind. Thomas went through it in the hope of finding a note, a receipt, or something else to indicate where the husband was holding Ellen prisoner.

But he found nothing. After hours of combing through the entire house, crying while thinking about what he had lost, wanting desperately to get it all back again, he finally left the house and went back to his flat.

The next day, he took the car and drove around town to see if he could find any trace of Ellen. He cruised slowly around in all the residential neighborhoods, looking for moving lorries, boxes in the front garden, anything indicating that someone had just moved in. He stopped at a house where the front garden was a mess and a moving lorry was parked outside. He observed the house all day until the owners came home. It wasn't Ellen or her husband, so he drove off.

Now it was almost a month since he had last seen Ellen and, as the days passed, he felt more and more sick. He was throwing up at night and could hardly eat during the day. He felt like his body had given up. Without his beloved, it simply refused to function. He still observed the house from across the road. A new family had moved in. A couple with two children, a young boy and a teenage girl. Rasmussen was their last name. Thomas had been observing the woman Lisa for several days in a row, but somehow it just wasn't the same. She wasn't the same. She wasn't Ellen. He kept comparing her to Ellen, and she kept falling short. Lisa was pregnant and about to give birth any day now. But she wasn't nearly as radiant as Ellen had been when she carried both her children, and Lisa didn't carry the baby as elegantly as Ellen had done. She was fit, yes, but clumsy and not graceful the way Ellen had been. Lisa was obsessed with cleaning and eating healthily; Ellen had never been any of that. As a matter of fact, Thomas grew more and more annoyed with this Lisa person as the days passed, simply because she wasn't anything like Ellen and she could never replace her, no matter how badly he wanted her to. He started fantasizing about killing her, about stabbing her, and yelling at her how incredibly ANNOYING she was and that he was doing the world a favor by removing her from the planet. He wanted to tell her she could never be anything like Ellen, that she could never take her place.

Thomas looked out the window and spotted the postal carrier as he approached Ellen's old mailbox. Then it struck him. If anyone knew where Ellen was, it had to be the postal carrier. He would know her new address, wouldn't he? Knowing their local postal carrier, Thomas knew he would definitely know. He knew where everybody lived on the island and he knew where to send Ellen's letters.

Thomas grabbed his hammer, stormed down the stairs, and waited till the postal carrier entered Thomas's building.

"Well, hello there, Thomas," the postal carrier said when he spotted him. The door shut behind him.

"Hi there," Thomas said, then lifted the hammer in the air and knocked the postal carrier out.

He dragged him upstairs to his flat where he tied him to a chair and waited for him to wake up. When he finally did, Thomas pulled out his toenails one by one with a pair of pliers, until he finally gave him the new address. Thomas swung the hammer again and killed the postal carrier with one stroke.

Then he set fire to his flat and drove off into the night.

THIRTY-FOUR
NOVEMBER 2013

Nora felt something touch her skin and opened her eyes. Then she screamed. It was dark and something was on her face. It felt like it was licking her. Nora screamed again. What was this? An animal of some sort? She tried to knock it off with her fists and it left, sounding like it flew off. Nora moaned in pain. Her body was hurting so terribly. What had happened to her? She tried to see, but it was so dark where she was. Once again, an animal touched her on her back. Its claws scratched the skin. Nora screamed again and moved around to get it off of her.

A light came on, and Nora could finally see where she was. She blinked her eyes quickly to try to focus. What was this place? A garage? And what was it that she was in? A cage of some sort? Nora finally managed to focus correctly and spotted twenty or thirty bats hanging from the ceiling.

Nora gasped. She hated bats. No it was more than that. She loathed them and was terrified of them. Had they been on her body? Had they been licking her face? Nora touched her lip and smeared blood on her fingers. She could hardly move her body because of the excruciating pain she was in. She tried to sit up. She could hardly remember what had happened to her and tried to recall the night before.

I remember being in my bed and not being able to sleep. Then I walked in to check on the baby and then... then outside in the hallway I heard something...

"Lisa!" she said out loudly. "Lisa?" she yelled. "Are you here?"

"No, but I am," another voice said.

Nora looked in the direction of the voice and spotted a man. He was walking closer to the cage she was in.

"Who... wh... who are you?" she asked.

"Does it matter who I am?" he asked with a grin.

"Why are you keeping me in here?"

The man laughed. He kneeled next to the cage and looked at her like she was an animal. "Because I can," he said.

"Please let me out of here. I'm terrified of bats."

"Are you now? Well, isn't that just peachy?"

"What do you mean? Why have you brought me here?" she asked, trying to pull herself up by the wire fence.

The man looked at Nora like he was examining her. "Some bad bruises you got there. I could hardly recognize you when I found you. Did that bastard of a husband do this to you? Did Erik beat you up again, huh, Nora?"

"How do you know my name? How do you know my husband's name? Who are you? Why are you doing this to me?"

"Back to the whys again, are we? I thought we covered that," the man said. "Do try to keep up here, Nora."

"What? I don't understand. Please, just let me out of here." Nora pleaded desperately. "Where is Lisa? Did she put you up to this or what is going on? Lisa? Where are you? It's not funny anymore."

The man sighed. "Do try to move on, Nora. Lisa is not here. And we're already behind schedule, so we'll have to move slightly faster; I hope you realize that."

"What schedule? What are you talking about?" Nora asked, feeling tired and confused.

"My schedule. I was supposed to already have you yesterday afternoon. I was waiting for you in the parking lot, but you weren't alone when you came out, were you? So I had to get you in your house instead. I had to risk so much for you, Nora. Just because that guy was with you. That Tim fellow. Yeah, I watched you two meet up in the alley behind the café. I saw him kiss you. Both of you are pretty pleased with the fact that I killed his wife, aren't you? Now you can finally be alone, huh? It's what you wanted isn't it? Both of you. Well, too bad, that is not going to happen either."

"You're the one who killed Simone?" Nora gasped. "Who are you? How do you know about me and Tim?"

The man giggled loudly. "Let's just say I've been watching you."

THIRTY-FIVE
NOVEMBER 2013

"The woman is still alive."

Morten sounded tired on the phone. I was sitting in front of my laptop working on my book when he called.

"The woman you pulled out of the car last night is stable. The doctor just called from the hospital. She is in a coma, but they think she might survive."

I leaned back on the couch filled with such a relief. "Boy, am I glad to hear that. Who is she?"

"Her name is Susanne Arnholm. She's a local girl from Nordby. She has two children. A man found her baby in a parking lot inside her car the day before yesterday. He called the police, and my colleague Allan, who was on duty, went to Susanne's house and found her other kid home alone. She had walked home from school when her mother didn't show up. Apparently, there is no husband. He died a year ago. Allan knows Susanne's mother who lives nearby and he took the children to her."

"Oh, my God. Are the children all right? How long was the baby in the car?" I asked.

"I don't know. But my guess is someone kidnapped Susanne

from the parking lot. I can see no other explanation to why the baby would end up alone in the car."

"You've got a point. What's frightening is that it's just like in the other case. They found that baby in the car as well, didn't they? In a parking lot?"

"Yes," Morten said.

"Is someone targeting mothers?" I asked.

Morten sighed. "It sure sounds like it, doesn't it? There's no doubt it's the same guy. Susanne was covered in animal bites and shot three times as well. In the shoulder, in the leg, and in her back. My guess is the killer thought she was dead before he drove her into the water."

"Was the car stolen too?" I asked.

"Yes. Just like before. The car was a Land Rover also. It was stolen a month ago somewhere outside of Aarhus."

"A month ago, huh? Someone has been planning this for quite some time."

"Yes. So it seems."

"What about the plumber? Any news about him?" I asked and spotted Sophia through my kitchen window. She was crossing the road with her baby in a sling on her stomach. She seemed upset as she was walking toward my house.

"No, nothing. But as long as he doesn't turn up in a car in the water, I assume he has nothing to do with this."

"Could he already be in there at the bottom of the sea?"

Morten exhaled. "I... I really hope not. We're still searching for him. I'm actually trying to track down his whereabouts today. It would be great to rule him out as one of this killer's victims."

"He doesn't quite fit the profile of the others," I said and walked toward the door when Sophia came closer.

"No, he doesn't. You've got that right. But get this. Another woman has been reported missing this morning. This time it's someone I know very well. Nora Willumsen is her name. She works here at the station as an assistant. Her husband reported her missing this morning. She was in bed last night, he said, but this morning she was gone and hadn't taken the baby with her. He found blood on the kitchen floor and we have someone out there looking at it right now. The problem is, the husband is known to slap her around every now and then, so if something happened to her, he is our main suspect, the bastard."

"Nora?" I asked, startled. "I think I know her."

"Well, if you see her, then please let us know. I really don't want any more of these women ending up in the ocean at night. Listen, I gotta run. Busy day here at the station. Everybody was called in today. Even Tim, the poor creature. Well, at least it was good news about Susanne Arnholm. Back to work. Talk to you later."

I hung up just as Sophia stormed through the door to my house.

"Susanne Arnholm was the woman in your mothers' group, right? The one who didn't show up yesterday at the hairdresser, right?"

Sophia looked at me without blinking. "Yes, she is, why? Is she dead?"

I shook my head. Sophia breathed in relief. "No," I said. "But she is in a coma at the hospital in Esbjerg. Someone shot her and tried to drown her, just like Simone." I paused and gazed at her. Baby Alma was sleeping heavily in the sling. "Nora is in your group too, isn't she? Nora Willumsen who works at the police station?"

Sophia nodded and put her diaper bag down on the floor. "Yeah. She's the one who hardly ever says anything. Why?"

"Well, I have a feeling someone is targeting members of your mothers' group. Nora went missing this morning."

Sophia looked like her heart had stopped. "What are you saying?"

"First it was Simone who was killed, right? Then Susanne

was shot but survived. Now Nora is missing? The only connection between them is the fact that they all have babies and they're in the same group as you."

Sophia sat down on one of my kitchen chairs with a sigh. "You've got to be kidding me."

"I might be wrong, but it is kind of strange, don't you think?"

"But why? Why would anyone target us? We're just a bunch of women with babies."

I grabbed a chair next to Sophia and sat down. "That's what we need to find out. Who else is in your group?"

"Lisa. Lisa Rasmussen. She and I are the only ones left."

"I guess we better talk to her then."

THIRTY-SIX
NOVEMBER 2013

Lisa didn't sleep all night. Frustrated with how it had all ended, she decided to clean the entire kitchen once she got back from Nora's place. Then she grabbed some meat from the freezer and started cooking. The stew was still boiling on the cooker when she heard Margrethe fuss upstairs. She ran up and grabbed her, changed her diaper, and tickled her tummy. Downstairs again, she gave Margrethe a bottle and put her in her playpen, then prepared breakfast while wondering what had happened to Nora. Had the burglar taken her to the hospital? Had he seen Lisa? Was this going to become a problem for her? She shook her head while putting more bread in the toaster. No, why would a burglar do that? Was he another secret lover? One she had made plans to meet with in the middle of the night? Why would she do that in her own house and risk getting caught? No, it didn't make any sense. Who was he? Lisa knew she had seen him somewhere... in the café. That was it. Yes, he was often a guest at Café Mimosa, her favorite.

Christian came down for breakfast. In a line behind him followed Jacob and Amalie. As usual, they were all in a hurry and had no time to chat or hardly to eat. They swallowed their food quickly. Amalie, who had piano practice, simply grabbed a piece of fruit and was out of the house.

"You need real food," Lisa yelled after her, but she was long gone.

"I have to get going," Christian said and washed down a bite of toast with coffee. He looked at Jacob. He had promised to take him to his office today, like he often did on Saturdays. "Ready, buddy?"

"Give him a chance to eat," Lisa said.

"I'm late, Lisa. If you had a real job you'd understand. I have a boss who wanted me at the office half an hour ago. You know we're working with an important client, and I have to be a team player and pitch in, even on weekends and holidays. We can't all just goof around. Come on, Jacob. Grab your jacket and let's go."

Jacob took one last bite of his toast with jam before he got up and grabbed his jacket. He looked at Lisa with a smile. "See you, Mom."

Christian leaned over and kissed Lisa on the cheek. "See you for dinner; it won't be late."

When the door closed, Lisa stared at all the food she had prepared that they had barely touched. Margrethe was babbling from the playpen. Lisa shook her head and started cleaning up.

I'll tell you who is goofing around. Running for city council is a job, mister. I'll show you. I am gonna show everybody.

The doorbell rang. Lisa screamed in frustration, then threw the dishes back in the sink. She walked to the door and opened it violently.

If it's another ignorant plumber...

"What?"

Outside stood an ugly-faced man. He smiled and held a badge up in the air. "Morten Bredballe, Nordby police. Could we have a word?"

Lisa looked at the badge. It looked fake. So did he.

"Could I come in?" he asked.

Lisa found her unbeatable election smile. "Sure. Come on in, officer."

"Thank you."

Lisa stepped aside and let the man enter her house, leaving muddy footprints behind him in the hallway. Lisa growled behind his back, then slammed the door shut.

"Should we do this in the kitchen?" he asked.

"Why not? It's all dirty anyway," Lisa said and walked ahead of him trying to make sure he followed her and didn't leave mud from his shoes anywhere else.

Calm down, Lisa. Floors can be cleaned. No need to get angry. Calm yourself down. Think about something nice. Picture the ocean, a meadow, a forest. There you go. Now remain calm, no matter what. You can do it.

"Would you like a cup of coffee, officer?" Lisa asked.

"Yes, that would be great. Thank you."

"Well, you're very welcome. It's the least I can do for our friends in uniform." Lisa grabbed a cup from the cupboard, then poured some coffee in it and placed it on the table in front of the fake officer.

Don't think I haven't figured you out with that toy badge of yours. What are you? Polish? Ukrainian? Come here to rob me, have you? To take advantage of a poor lonely woman home alone? Did you stand outside and watch as my husband left so you knew I'd be alone? Come to steal my money? My credit cards and silverware? My flat-screen TV and my iPad and sell them on the black market? Well, you're in for a little surprise, my good friend. Oh, how you're in for a surprise.

THIRTY-SEVEN
FEBRUARY 2013

Thomas had butterflies in his stomach as he drove through town. Behind him his old building stood in flames, and in the distance, he could hear blaring sirens. He enjoyed looking at the flames in the rearview mirror while driving out of town and into the countryside. He couldn't help being a little proud of himself. He was a genius, really. Leaving the body of the postal carrier in the flat was a stroke of genius. It really was. Once the firefighters put out the fire and they found the remains of the body, it would be so burned that they wouldn't be able to see it wasn't Thomas. They were going to think he was dead. And the way things were right now in his life, that suited Thomas more than anything.

He had written the address on a small piece of paper. He looked at it, feeling so excited. He couldn't wait to see Ellen again. When she woke up tomorrow morning, he would be close to her. And this time, he wasn't going to let go of her again. Never again. Never.

Till death parts us.

Thomas found the address easily. It turned out it was out in the country. A small farm outside of Nordby. Not even half an hour's drive away.

All this time you've been so close, dear Ellen. And I didn't know. Maybe you tried to tell me, maybe I just didn't listen. I promise it won't happen again. I promise. I'll stay close from now on, never let you out of my sight.

Thomas parked the car not far away, then ran up the dirt road toward the house. It was dark and all the lights were out, making the place seem abandoned, but Thomas knew it wasn't. Somewhere in there behind those walls was his beloved. He knew she was. He could sense she was close. It felt so good to finally be in her presence again, to be close.

Thomas tiptoed around the house and peeked in through all the windows to see if he could spot her. Just catch a glimpse of his beloved whom he had missed so deeply for weeks now.

"Where are you, Ellen?" he whispered with so much joy he had a hard time containing it.

Finally he found her. Thomas breathed in a deep breath as he spotted her through a crack in the curtains that hadn't been closed all the way. The light from the full moon outside hit her face and made her look like an angel.

Thomas almost cried with happiness. Oh, this lovely sight. How he adored watching her. How he worshipped her. The most perfect creature on the face of the earth.

Next to her, the handsome husband turned in his sleep and put his arm around Ellen. Thomas felt a pinch of rage in his heart. How he loathed the man who had come between them. How he despised him for keeping them apart, for holding Ellen captive against her will. Wasn't there some law against that? Couldn't the police see what was really going on?

Thomas clenched his fists while watching them. He had to restrain himself. He wanted to run in there so badly and beat the crap out of that husband of hers.

Why did you marry that bastard, Ellen? Why? What did you see in him anyway? Did he force you? What has he been doing to you? Has he hurt you? If he has, I swear to God, I'm gonna hurt him too.

Just as Thomas finished the thought, the handsome husband opened his eyes like he had heard him. He stared directly at Thomas.

Thomas didn't hide himself. He lifted his clenched fist and showed it to the husband without realizing it was smeared in the postal carrier's blood. So were his clothes. Thomas looked at the husband until he opened his mouth and started screaming. Then Thomas ran. He ran as fast as he could down the dirt road, through the small forest and jumped inside of his car that was parked on the big road. Then he drove off.

THIRTY-EIGHT
NOVEMBER 2013

The strange man kept staring at Nora in the cage. She had no idea what to do and was too sore and beaten up to care. She was lying on the newspapers on the floor, whimpering and moaning in pain. What the hell was going on here? What was Lisa up to? Why was she doing this to her? Had she hired this guy to hurt her?

"What do you want from me?" she moaned.

The man was squatting in front of the cage and had been for a very long time. Nora thought he looked like he was speculating over something. He hadn't uttered a word for a long time now.

"Please just let me out. I want to go home to my baby." Finally, he spoke. "You won't."

"What? What are you saying? What is it you want from me? Why are you keeping me here?" she cried.

"I'm keeping you here because you deserve no better."

"I haven't done anything to you," she said.

"Oh, but that's where you're wrong. You have. You have done something to me. Something unforgivable."

Nora wailed. "I don't even know you. How can I have done

something to you? How? Is this Lisa's doing? Did she put you up to this?"

The man smiled. "Could you be quiet for once? I'm trying to think."

"Think? Think about what?"

"I'm figuring out how best to kill you."

"What?"

"You heard me. Can you even stand up straight?" he asked.

Nora lifted her head. It hurt so badly. She grabbed the fence and pulled herself up till she was standing. Her sore body hurt like crazy. The wound on her hand was pounding where Lisa had pierced it with the knife.

"Oh, good, you can," the man smiled. "Now try to move."

"Why?"

The man clenched his fists and closed his eyes. "Just do it, will you? Please?"

Nora drew in a deep breath, then took a step forward. Her legs felt fine but she was extremely dizzy from all the blows she had suffered to her head.

"Good," the man said and clapped his hands. "Now walk a little more."

Nora kept walking while holding on to the fence. The bats seemed disturbed and started moving around.

"Can I please sit down now?" Nora asked.

"Not yet. I need to know that you can walk without holding on to the fence," the man said.

"Why? I'm so tired. Please just let me sleep," Nora pleaded.

"Just show me that you can."

"Will you leave me alone then?" Nora asked.

The man chuckled. "Even better."

"What could be better?" Nora asked.

The man chuckled again. "I could... let's see... oh, I've got it. What if I promised that if you can walk over to the end of the cage and back without holding on, I'll let you out of the cage?"

Nora opened her eyes widely. "You'd do that? You'd let me out of the cage?" she asked, her voice filled with hope.

The man nodded slowly. "I promise. Cross my heart and hope to die."

Nora was panting with happiness and expectation. Could it be? Could it really be that he would let her out, let her go home? She took in a deep breath, then let go of the fence and started walking... carefully, so she wouldn't fall and he wouldn't be able to use that as an excuse for not keeping his word to her. She put one foot in front of the other and managed to take the first step. The other leg followed and soon she was walking without a problem to the end, then she turned and walked back.

"Ta-da," she said, her voice shivering.

"Very good," the man laughed.

Nora looked at him waiting for him to say that now he wasn't going to let her out after all, but much to her surprise, he kept his promise and unlocked the door to the cage and helped her out. Nora laughed with relief when he closed the door after her and locked it. Finally, she was out. Finally, she wouldn't have to worry about those disgusting bats. Her face was still hurting from where they had been sitting and licking the blood off of her wounds.

"So why did you have to see if I could walk before you let me out?" she asked.

The man laughed again. "Because, *dearie...* I wanted to make sure you could run."

THIRTY-NINE
NOVEMBER 2013

I tried to call Morten on my phone, but he didn't answer. Sophia was sitting in my kitchen biting her nails and swilling down one cup of coffee after another.

"I'm sorry," I said and turned to her. "He's not answering."

"I'm really scared, Emma," Sophia said.

"I know, sweetie. I'll try again in a little while. He is probably just working. He told me they had a busy day."

"So you finally slept with him, huh?" she asked.

I shook my head and sipped my coffee. I grabbed a biscuit. Sophia hadn't touched them. It concerned me. She was usually as bad as me when it came to sweets. "No. Actually we just spent the night together, but nothing happened. We kissed a lot though."

"Wow," Sophia said. "He didn't even try anything?"

"Well, it was kind of not in question. We had just pulled a woman from a car and were almost freezing to death. He only stayed to keep me warm."

"Yeah, right," Sophia grunted.

"Besides he was too frozen to do anything," I chuckled.

"Ah, that must be the explanation," Sophia said with a

nervous grin. I hated seeing her anxious like this. It was so unlike her.

"You know what?" I asked as I put the half-eaten biscuit down on the table.

"What?"

"I am gonna call the police station and ask them to send someone over to protect you. We can't wait for Morten to pick up his phone."

Sophia nodded. "I'd like that. I'd naturally prefer Morten, but right now, anyone would do."

I picked up the phone and called the police station. I talked to Allan, whom I had met a couple of times when I went down there to do research for my book. I told him my concern. He went quiet.

"I'm sorry," he said. "We simply don't have enough officers to have one guard Sophia's house all day. But we do have a car on the streets right now. I can have them swing by your neighborhood and have them stay nearby. Except if anything happens elsewhere. Then they'll have to go. Will that do?"

"I think it will," I said and hung up.

"They're sending a patrol," I said making it sound like it was a bigger deal than it was. "They'll be here sometime soon."

Sophia breathed, relieved. "That's good," she said. "At least it will provide some safety for me and the kids. Could I stay here at your house for the rest of the day?"

"Stay all night if you want. I have plenty of rooms upstairs you can crash in and enough for the kids as well. They know the house."

"Are you kidding? They love your house," Sophia exclaimed. "Are you sure it's okay? My mom took them yesterday and will bring them back later today."

"I would be happy to have all of you here. It would make me calmer to be able to keep an eye on you myself."

Sophia lit up. "You're the best. You know that don't you?"

I chuckled. "I guess I do. Biscuit?"

"Yes, please," Sophia said and grabbed two. She ate greedily and started to look more like herself again. "But what about Lisa?" she asked with her mouth full.

I sighed. "Do you want me to bring her here too?"

Sophia looked terrified. "I would love it if we could avoid it, but maybe it's the right thing to do. To tell you the truth, I can't stand the woman. She is so obsessive. Perfectionistic to the extreme. She'll hate it here in all the mess."

"You think my house is messy?" I asked, startled. This coming from a woman whose house looked like it had been bombed.

"No, I think it is cozy and I love it here, but it's not clinically clean like Lisa's house. Not even the hospitals are as clean as her house. It's awful. We only met at her place once and it was horrible. She kept running after us, cleaning the floor where we had walked and disinfecting everything our kids touched. She was a nervous wreck. After that, we decided to avoid her house from then on, because we didn't want to put her or ourselves through that ever again. So whenever she suggests that we meet at her house, we always come up with an excuse or something else to do instead. It has worked so far."

"Well, she did come off as kind of obnoxious," I said and looked out the kitchen window. "The patrol is here," I said.

Sophia looked relieved.

"He won't dare to come close now that they're here," I said and walked to the door. I spoke to one of the officers and told them that Sophia would be in my house the rest of the day and night. They agreed to stay nearby and keep a close watch on my house.

I returned to Sophia, who was finishing off my biscuits in the kitchen. "So what do we do about this Lisa then?" I asked.

FORTY

FEBRUARY 2013

"I know what I saw," the handsome husband grumbled.

Ellen was sitting at the kitchen table in their new home hiding her face between her hands. "But Mads. It can't be. It couldn't have been him," she said.

They had been discussing him for hours. Thomas was watching them from outside the window, mostly listening while sitting with his back against the wall beneath the open kitchen window.

"He was there, Ellen. I saw him. He was looking at us while we were sleeping. And he was covered in blood."

"How could you even see that if it was in the middle of the night? It was dark," Ellen said, with tears in her voice.

"There was a full moon. I've told you this a million times the last three days. The light from the moon hit his face, and I saw blood on his hands and cheek. The man is dangerous, Ellen."

"He saved Gerda's life, remember?" Ellen said. Thomas felt a pinch of happiness in his heart. Ellen was defending him. It had to be a sign.

"Yes. I remember. How could I ever forget?" Mads said with

a deep sigh. "And I am grateful for that, but I think he is dangerous. That's why we moved, remember? He made you feel very uncomfortable, or has that changed all of a sudden? Have you taken a liking to him suddenly? Maybe there is something you haven't told me after all? 'Cause I have always found it strange that a guy would become obsessed with a woman he didn't even know, Ellen. When are you going to tell me the truth about him?"

Ellen moaned. "Not that again. We have been through this a million times, Mads. I never knew the guy. I have no idea why he has become obsessed with me. I don't know why... I swear to God, I don't have a clue. You have to believe me, Mads. Or I swear I'm gonna lose it."

"So he wasn't your lover? You didn't sleep with him while we were married or something?"

"How could you even ask such a horrible thing?" Ellen said furiously. Thomas felt her frustration and hoped she would finally leave her husband. He knew she wanted to, but he didn't understand what she was waiting for. Maybe she was afraid of him. Afraid of what her husband might do.

"It's just really hard to understand, Ellen. You have to realize that."

"Don't you think I know that? Don't you think I feel exactly the same way? This guy has been stalking me for what, almost ten years now? Don't you think I think about it every day, asking why he chose me, of all people? Don't you think I'm asking myself that very question every day?"

Mads exhaled deeply. "I know, Ellen. I know. It's just... just so hard. I thought we would finally get rid of him when we moved, you know. I thought this was it. Now we could move on with our lives. And then this."

"But it couldn't have been him, Mads," Ellen said. "The police told us he was dead when I called them. He died in his flat, probably suicide, they said. They found the burned remains of him inside the flat. He is gone, Mads. It must have been a dream. Your mind is playing tricks or something."

Mads exhaled again. "I know what they told you, but I'm telling you he is still out there. He is alive, and he has found us. I can't believe you refuse to believe me. After all we've been through," Mads said.

They both went quiet, then a door slammed. Thomas smiled from under the window. He had been living in his car ever since he got there. He followed Ellen wherever she went and watched her sleep at night, never taking his eyes off of her for more than a few hours when he needed to get some sleep himself. Being close to her again made him calmer, and he finally felt whole, but it wasn't quite enough anymore. He wanted more, he needed more than this.

Thomas sighed and rubbed his eyes. He had developed a tic in one eye that bothered him, especially when he felt agitated. He had trouble controlling his mind. The lack of sleep didn't help much, but he felt like he was slowly losing grip of reality, of what was real and what was fantasy. It felt like he was slipping. He kept imagining killing the handsome husband, and there were days when he thought he had already done so. The many voices in his head wouldn't keep quiet about it and, at times, he thought the only way to make them shut up was to obey.

FORTY-ONE
NOVEMBER 2013

"So what can I do for you, Officer... Bredballe, was it?"

Lisa pulled out a smoothie from the refrigerator that she had made earlier in the morning and started drinking it while staring at the fake officer. She felt like she had seen him before and wondered for a second if she was wrong about him, if he really did work at the station downtown. Lisa had never had much to do with the local officers. And she wasn't going to start to now. The guy was sloppy and dirty and highly annoying.

"Yes. Morten Bredballe," he said. "You're new in town?"

"Yes, been here about a year now."

"How do you like it?"

"We love it," Lisa said with a huge smile.

The officer smiled back and sipped his coffee while staring at the smoothie in her hand. "Meat smoothie," she said. "With beetroot. Very high in protein. I have more, would you like to try one?"

The officer looked like he was about to throw up.

How rude, Lisa thought.

"No, thanks. The reason I'm here is actually to ask you about a man who went missing a couple of days ago. His name is Bo Quist. He works for Nordby VVS. It's a plumbing company. On the morning he went missing, he was supposed to have come here. He had another client before you and he showed up for them, but that's where the trail ends."

Lisa drank her smoothie through the straw. She didn't even blink when the officer mentioned the plumber. Simply because she didn't care.

She shrugged. "That's most unfortunate, officer, but I can't say I've seen him. We haven't seen a plumber in this house at all and it's been weeks since we called the company. WEEKS. Can't say I'm impressed with them, but they're the only ones in town I understand."

"Well, yes. That is true. So are you telling me that Bo Quist never came here at all?" the officer asked and put a picture of the plumber on the table for Lisa to look at. She shook her head with a chuckle.

"No, anyone that ugly, I would remember," she said.

The officer stared at her, then down at the picture. "We did find his lorry parked downtown," he said. "So he must have gone down there after the former client and whatever happened to him after that remains a mystery."

Lisa sucked up the last remains of her meat smoothie through the straw and made a loud sucking noise. She put the empty glass on the table, then looked at the officer and smiled. "It sure does," she said, wondering if she should use the knife and stab him in the chest, or if she could come up with something a little more fun this time. The knife thing was getting old. "And even worse. Our sink is still broken."

"Well, yes. That is unfortunate. Say, you don't happen to know Nora Willumsen, by any chance. She has a baby about the same age as yours."

"I know Nora. Yes. She is in my mothers' group. Can't say I know her well though."

The officer nodded. Lisa turned her head and looked at the

knife on the table. She hadn't had time to clean it properly. Then she spotted the carving fork and a smile planted itself across her face. It wasn't her election smile; no, this smile was different.

"Well, the thing is, Nora Willumsen has disappeared as well," the officer continued.

Lisa stared at the officer thinking that maybe he wasn't fake after all; maybe he wasn't here to attack her and take her jewelry. He seemed too well informed to be fake. Lisa put her hand on the carving fork and caressed it gently. The officer stared at her. She felt his eyes on her body. Was he checking her out? Or was he on to her? Either way, he annoyed her immensely. But worst of all were those dirty boots. Lisa looked at her nice wooden floors that she had just cleaned. Smeared in mud.

Smeared. Defiled. Tainted.

Lisa lifted her eyes and met his. "But I take it you haven't seen her either," he said and wrote something on his notepad.

Lisa shook her head slowly. "No, officer. I haven't seen her either. Not since we were at the hairdresser yesterday. Boy, a lot of people have gone missing lately, haven't they?"

The officer sighed. "Yes. I..." he stopped and looked at her. "Did you say that Nora was in your mothers' group?"

"Yes," Lisa said and picked up the carving fork in her hand. It felt heavy. She wondered how it was going to sound once she pierced it through his chest. How deep would it go? Would it pierce through his lungs? Would she be able to pierce it straight through his heart or would she have to stab him again and again to kill him? She preferred the last one. She loved to get rid of all her frustrations in that manner.

"Who else is in that group? Was Simone Beaumont in it as well?"

"Yes, as a matter of fact, she was." Lisa walked closer with the carving fork clenched in her hand.

"What about Susanne Arnholm?"

"Part of the group too," Lisa said, walking close to him. He didn't seem to notice. He was lost in his own chain of thoughts.

Let me give you something to think about, sweetheart. Let me help you forget about everything else around you.

Lisa closed her eyes and went to that special place, the place of pure pleasure and delight, before opening them again. She looked at her victim, her prey, with a grin, then lifted the fork into the air, when the sound of the doorbell made her lose her momentum and the arm with the fork dropped down behind the officer's back instead of inside of him.

"Who the hell is that?" she growled and sprang for the door. "What?" she yelled and opened it, still clenching the carving fork in her hand.

"Hi, Lisa," a woman standing outside said.

"Who the hell are you?"

"I'm Emma. We met at the hairdresser yesterday, remember? I'm Sophia's friend."

FORTY-TWO
NOVEMBER 2013

"Emma. That's right. Now I remember you."

Lisa looked a little manic when she talked. I wondered if she was all right. Maybe she had already heard about Nora and put the pieces together.

"Come on in," she said, and made room for me to walk past her. Remembering what Sophia had told me, I stopped in the hallway and took off my boots. Lisa saw it and smiled.

"Thank you," she said. "I've just cleaned."

"Well, I know how boots can leave dirty marks all over the place. Especially at this time of year when it rains a lot and there's mud everywhere outside."

Lisa tilted her head and smiled again. "That is so true," she said. "Not many people realize this. But it is so true."

I smiled and nodded, sensing that Lisa had taken a liking to me. "Come into the kitchen," she said. "Can I get you anything?"

I looked at her and was about to refuse, but I realized that she was the type who would be offended if I said no. "I'd love some coffee if you have any."

"Coffee it is," she said, chirping.

I followed her into the kitchen. She placed the carving fork I had noticed in her hand when she opened the door on the counter, then went for the coffeemaker. To my surprise, she wasn't alone. Morten was in the kitchen.

"Emma," he said, looking at me startled. "What on earth are you doing here?"

"I'm here to talk to Lisa. What are you doing here?" For a split second I felt the spirit of jealousy visit my heart. I couldn't help but wonder what he was doing in another woman's kitchen. But then I noticed the notepad on the table and the pen in his hand, and I blushed. Of course, he was just working.

"I'm here on a police matter," he said with a shy smile.

"Why, isn't this nice?" Lisa chirped and clapped her hands. "You two know each other."

"It's good that you are here," I said, ignoring Lisa's sarcastic remark. "I've been trying to reach you. You should hear this."

I sat down while Lisa put a cup of coffee in front of me. I sipped it while Lisa sat down as well. She seemed like she couldn't relax. Like having us in her kitchen made her highly uncomfortable. A small flat-screen TV was on in the corner of the kitchen showing the local Fanoe TV station. It had been muted. Lisa stared up at it, then back at me.

"So what is it that is so important?" she asked.

"Well, I'm afraid you might be in danger," I said.

Lisa looked at me, then laughed out loud. "Me? Now that's a new one. And why, might I ask, do you believe I am in *danger*?" She said, sounding like she was mocking me.

"It's the mothers' group," Morten said.

"Exactly," I said. "I believe the killer is targeting your mothers' group. Three people have disappeared; all were part of the group. Two of them turned up in cars in the ocean. Both of them were shot. Only one survived."

"And now Nora has disappeared as well," Morten said.

"That leaves only you and Sophia," I continued.

"Where is Sophia?" Morten asked.

"Back at my house with Alma who is asleep. I called your station. There's a patrol keeping an eye on her and the neighborhood."

"Good," he said.

"Now I say we get Lisa back with us as well. What do you say, Lisa?" I said and turned to look at her. But Lisa seemed to have lost interest in the conversation. She was staring at the flat-screen TV in the corner where a man was being interviewed.

"Per Egon, candidate for city council," the text said beneath him.

"Lisa?" Morten said.

She still didn't answer. She walked closer to the TV and turned up the sound. I looked at Morten and shrugged. Lisa seemed lost in what was going on inside the TV. The voice of Per Egon filled the kitchen.

"Yes, I do believe my opponent Lisa Rasmussen should withdraw right away," he said.

"And why is that?"

"I hold here evidence that she is a fake," Per Egon said and held a piece of paper up in the air for the camera to see.

"And what exactly are we looking at?" the journalist asked.

Per Egon grinned. "This is proof that Lisa Rasmussen never passed her final exam at business school in Karrebaeksminde, as she claims to have. This proves she is a fake, a phony, and no one should vote for her. After all, if this isn't true, what else is she lying about?"

I got up from the chair. "Lisa... ? We really should take this seriously. You should come to my house where we will be able to protect you. You'll have to deal with that other stuff later. Right now, it's your safety that's important. Have your family come over as well, just to make sure."

Lisa was frozen. Her back was still turned to me and

Morten. I walked closer and realized she was shivering. I put a hand on her shoulder.

"Lisa..."

"That son of a..." she mumbled. "I'll show him who is fake, I'll show him. I will. I have to..." Lisa turned and looked into my eyes. She seemed lost in her own thoughts. I had a feeling she hadn't listened to anything I'd said.

"Lisa? Will you come to my house?" I asked again.

"It's a great idea," Morten said. "You should do it, Lisa. There is no way we can send out a patrol to guard your house as well. This way you'll be protected."

Lisa mumbled something, then looked up.

"So what do you say?" I asked.

"What? Say to what?"

"To spending the night at my place?"

"Oh, that... well, I guess. I just have... I mean, I have something I need to do first," she said pensively.

"Okay," I said and looked at Morten. "Maybe I'll stay with you till you're done," I said.

Lisa turned her head like an owl and looked at me. "No! No. I don't need your help. I don't need anyone's protection. I'm fine, don't you see? I'm great. I'm perfect. I can take care of myself. Don't you worry about a thing."

Morten got up from the chair. "Lisa, you really should go."

Lisa nodded distantly while mumbling something about the carving fork. I was wondering if she was at all well.

"Yes, yes," she said. "I'll come over later." She grabbed my shoulder and pushed me slightly toward the front door, handing me my boots to put on. "Now, just leave. I'll be right there. Just have a small errand I need to run downtown."

"You really shouldn't be alone," Morten said. Lisa grabbed his shoulder and started pushing him as well.

"Oh, I won't be alone. Don't you worry about that. In fact, don't worry about me at all. I'm never alone. I have all the voices in my head to keep me company, ha ha," she said, chuckling while pushing us out the front door.

"Do take care now," she said and slammed the door in our faces.

I stared at Morten who shrugged with a smile. "Can't force her," he said. "If she doesn't want our protection."

"I know," I said and walked toward my car. Across the road, I spotted an abandoned building.

"What happened here?" I asked.

"There was a fire earlier in the year. Killed the man inside the top flat. They say he committed suicide because of unrequited love. It was never rebuilt."

"That's so sad."

"I know."

FORTY-THREE
MARCH 2013

Thomas was going through Ellen's drawers. They had left to go to the theater downtown and Thomas had decided to stay behind. He had followed them all the way there and watched them go inside before he drove back to the farm and broke in through the window in the basement.

Thomas found a pair of her underwear in the basket in the bathroom and sniffed them. He held them to his face and rubbed his nose in them. Oh, how amazing they smelled. How intoxicating.

He put the underwear in his pocket then moved on to the rest of the bedroom. He put his head on her pillow and sniffed it, then rubbed his own head on it, imagining he was hugging her and smelling her hair.

Soon, Ellen. Soon, we will be together. Soon, nothing will ever be able to come between us again.

"Who's in here?" The voice of the handsome husband shattered the air above Thomas. He rolled down to the floor, then rolled under the bed. Thomas was shivering as he heard the sound of the husband's big boots come closer.

"Hello?"

"There is no one here," Ellen said.

Thomas smiled. Her sweet voice always made him so happy.

"You're just being paranoid, Mads. I'll get the kids to bed."

The boots were outside the bedroom now. Then they stopped. Thomas heard Ellen talk to the children in the bathroom while they brushed their teeth. They were laughing. Thomas closed his eyes and enjoyed the sound of Ellen's laughter. It felt almost like he was there with her, laughing, goofing around with the kids.

It should have been you. This family should have been yours. Not his. He stole it from you. He stole your life, your future. It's time you take it back. It's time that you take back what is rightfully yours.

The door to the bedroom opened and the boots entered. A second later, a face looked directly at Thomas. Then an arm reached in under the bed, grabbed him, and pulled him out.

"Ha!" the husband yelled. "I knew you were still alive. I was right! Ellen, come and see what I've found."

Thomas was shivering and pulled out of the husband's grip. A kick from his boot made Thomas fall back to the floor in pain.

"Ellen!" the husband yelled again. "Come in here. Right now!"

Steps were coming closer and then they stopped. Thomas heard Ellen gasp, then whimper before she shooed the children back to their room. The husband kicked Thomas in the stomach a few times before Ellen finally returned.

"Stop!" she said. "He's bleeding."

The husband was panting. The kicks paused. Thomas coughed to breathe.

"What's the matter with you? Are you defending him again? Can't you see I was right?" the husband said.

"Yes. Yes, Mads. You were right, okay? But there is no reason to beat him," Ellen said.

"Why, Ellen? Can you give me one good reason for not beating the crap out of this creep? He has been harassing us for nearly ten years now. TEN years. Don't you think it is about time we taught him a lesson? The police won't do it because they believe he is dead, so it's up to us now, Ellen. This is our chance to tell him what we think of him and make him go away."

"Yes, you're right, but not this way," Ellen said. "Beating him is wrong. He did, after all..."

"If you say that he 'saved our daughter's life' one more time, I'm gonna scream," her husband interrupted her.

"Then scream all you want," Ellen said. "I don't care. Don't you understand he is sick?"

"That I can agree with. He is a sick bastard who deserves to be punished," the husband said, then lifted his clenched fist and slammed it into Thomas's face.

Thomas screamed in pain. Ellen yelled.

"Stop it. Stop it, Mads. I won't let you beat him anymore. There are other ways to do this."

"Is that so?" the husband said. "Like what?"

Ellen kneeled next to Thomas. He felt her touch his cheek gently. It felt so soothing. He closed his eyes and enjoyed her touch. She wiped off some blood, then looked at him. Oh, how Thomas had dreamed of this moment for so long.

This is it. It's finally here. The moment when Ellen tells you she loves you. Finally, she is going to let her husband know who her heart really belongs to. Finally, your time has come.

"Thomas?" Ellen said with such a gentle voice it almost made Thomas cry. "Thomas Hamilton, that's your name, right?"

Thomas was in pain but nodded anyway.

"All right, Thomas. Now listen to me..."

This is it. This is the moment in all the films when the hero finally gets the girl, when she says the words he has longed to hear.

Ellen had tears in her eyes as she looked at him. It moved him deeply. "Thomas..." she hesitated like she needed to find the courage. "For years and years now I have feared you. For years I thought you were harassing me and my family, but lately I have come to realize that you're not a bad person, Thomas. You're just a little confused. You believe I love you, but I really don't. I have a husband and a family, and I don't love you. I really don't. I hardly know you. You must realize now that you can't have me... ever. You'll never be with me. Do you understand that, Thomas? Do you?"

She might as well have beaten Thomas up herself. At that instant, he would have preferred that to this. It would have hurt less. Thomas moaned in pain and looked up at her.

"But... but, Ellen... I love you."

"I know you think you do, Thomas. I've read so much about this type of behavior lately, and I know that you think you love me, but you don't. It's an illusion, Thomas. It's not real."

"But we have so much together..." Thomas said, his voice shivering.

Ellen shook her head while Thomas sat up. He couldn't believe what she had just said. It was so painful; he couldn't understand how she could be so heartless.

"No, Thomas. We don't. We don't have anything together. What we have is not real. It's in your head. And I'm sorry that you have to go through this to understand it, but I have to tell you the truth. I have to be honest with you. I don't love you, Thomas. I don't. I love my husband. I love Mads and you need to understand that. You need to leave us alone."

Thomas got to his feet. Blood was running from his nose into his mouth. It tasted horrible.

"I love you, Ellen," he said again, hoping desperately that she would come to her senses and say the same to him.

"What's this?" the husband said and pulled something out of Thomas's pocket. It was the underwear.

The husband looked at the silky underwear, then at Ellen who gasped, appalled. "Still don't think he deserves a beating?"

Ellen took the underwear while looking at Thomas with disgust. "Do what you want," she said, then left.

"Ellen?" Thomas tried, while the husband picked up a rifle from the corner of the room.

"I've been sleeping with this next to my bed for years now, expecting to one night catch you in my house and shoot you," the husband said, while cocking the rifle. "I guess no one will miss you, huh?"

Thomas turned his head in search of a way out. Then, he jumped for the window smashing the glass as he went through. It hurt like hell as he landed on the ground, but still he managed to get up and start running while the husband took aim with the rifle.

"That's right, my friend," he yelled after him. "You better run. Run as fast as you can."

FORTY-FOUR
NOVEMBER 2013

Lisa was running. She was pushing baby Margrethe while she was sleeping in her stroller. Lisa was panting, not because of the effort as much as because of the agitation she felt inside. That bastard. Did he really think he would get away with smearing her on TV like that?

Not on my watch, mister. You're in for quite the surprise.

She had brought the carving fork. It was in her purse as she stormed across town pushing the stroller in front of her. Lisa was angry. No, she was beyond that. She was fuming, furious, on the verge of desperate. She was sweating and freezing all at once. The cold wind was hurting her cheeks, biting them, but she hardly noticed. Usually, she would be very anxious and make sure to protect her skin properly when outside in the wind, but not today.

Lisa ran around a corner, almost bumped into a man, cursed at him like a sailor, and continued. She spotted the building where Per Egon worked as a librarian. She didn't stop so she wouldn't seem suspicious; no, she ran even faster now that she could see the library building in front of her. The doors slid open and she stormed inside.

A short, fat woman with messy hair was sitting behind a counter. She stared at Lisa with wide-open eyes. "May I help you?"

"Where is he?" Lisa asked, still panting.

"Who?" the woman asked.

Pathetic little midget. Whom do you think I'm talking about?

"Per Egon. I need to see him," Lisa answered. "I have a very important matter to discuss with him."

"Ah, now I know where I've seen you before," the little person said. "You're that woman who is running for city council. I recognize you from the poster. Between you and me, I'm happy that you're running. We need more women in charge around here instead of all those old men."

Lisa forced her election smile to appear. "Yes, yes that's me. So where is he? Could you please be a dear and tell me where he is?"

The little person smiled. "Yeah, sure. He's in the back."

Lisa kept the smile on her lips. "Well, thank you so much. Now don't forget to vote." She pushed the stroller between the rows of books that soon hid her completely. It was a huge library, much to her surprise.

She found Per Egon all the way at the end. He was on a ladder, putting books back on the shelves. Lisa took in a deep breath to try to calm herself down.

"What do you want?" he asked without even looking at her. "Have you come to announce your withdrawal from the election?"

Lisa felt her cheeks burning. If it was the anger or meeting the sudden heat when she got inside from the cold, she didn't know.

"I most certainly am not withdrawing from anything," she snorted. "If you think you can scare me with your little lies, then you will be very surprised."

Per Egon turned his head and looked at Lisa. Then he

smiled. "Lies? That wasn't a lie. Facts don't lie. You never passed that exam."

Lisa shrugged. "So what?"

"So you're a liar."

"I'll just pass it at another time, what's it to you?"

Per Egon stared at Lisa like she was from Mars. "What are you talking about? You can't get elected if you lie to people."

Lisa scoffed again. "I really can't see why that should be a problem. Politicians lie all the time. It doesn't mean anything. I can still do a lot of good for this city and get it cleaned up."

Per Egon laughed, then climbed down the ladder with a book in his hand. Lisa let go of the stroller and put her hand in her purse. She caressed the carving fork inside of it with her fingers.

"Sweetie, if the public can't trust you, they won't elect you. It's that simple," Per Egon said, talking to her like she was a complete idiot. He walked closer to her than she cared for and stuck his face very close to hers. He was spitting while he spoke, his breath smelled like cheese and coffee. "They deserve to know the truth. That much I owe them. I'm sorry, but after this, I don't see how anyone would vote for you. Do you? Do you see it, Lisa? Why would anyone vote for you?"

"Because I'm the only one LEFT!" Lisa exclaimed, then pulled out the carving fork and plunged it into Per Egon's chest, pressing it in as deeply as she could, trying to make sure it hit something vital, preferably his heart.

FORTY-FIVE
NOVEMBER 2013

I was still worried about Lisa when I got back to the house. Sophia jumped out of her chair when I opened the door to the kitchen. She had baby Alma on her hip.

"How did it go?" she asked, and sat down with Alma in her lap.

I shrugged and sat down. "She sure is something, that Lisa."

"Yeah, I know," Sophia said, and shook her head. "She is not altogether there. I have been wondering about her. If she is mentally well, you know?"

"I know. But I told her to come here with her family later on. Now, we'll just have to see if she'll do it or not. At least we did what we could."

"That's true."

"Any news here?" I asked, and looked around. I could hear Sophia's kids in the living room playing.

Sophia shrugged. "Don't look at me. I'm hiding in here," she chuckled. "They came back fifteen minutes ago. My mom just threw them out and drove away in a hurry. I hope they won't tear your house apart."

"And where are Victor and Maya?" I asked.

"Maya is in the living room with the young ones. Victor stormed upstairs as soon as the little ones came into the garden. I don't think he's come down."

"Probably won't. Do you think your kids are hungry? I can easily bake something if you'd like."

Sophia exhaled. "That would be great. I bet they're starving and I have to feed the little one."

"Sure. No problem," I said.

Sophia made some porridge for Alma and fed her a couple of spoonfuls, which she spat out again, before she finally gave her a bottle of milk. I took out the dough I had prepared earlier and rolled it into buns that I placed in the oven.

"They'll be ready in half an hour. I'll go check on Victor," I said and trotted upstairs. I knocked on Victor's door and, when he didn't answer, I walked right in. He was sitting on the floor with his back against the wall, holding his hands to his ears, rocking back and forth. I felt a pinch in my stomach. I had forgotten to consider him when inviting all these people into our house. I kneeled next to him.

"Victor, sweetie?"

He looked at me. "There is a reason why the word noise means *unwanted sound*," he said. "According to the dictionary it's *a sound that is loud, unpleasant, unexpected, or undesired.*"

"I know it's very unpleasant for you, Victor, but what do you want me to do? Sophia is scared out of her mind because of this killer who wants to kill her and the other women from her mothers' group. The police are up to their ears in work and can't protect these women. I had to help them somehow. Especially Sophia, who is like family to us."

"Are you telling me there will be more?" Victor asked.

I exhaled with a smile. "Yes, sweetie. There might be another family coming. They only have three kids, as far as I am told."

"I'm not sharing my room with them. They should go to a

hotel. This is not a hotel. This is a house. The permissible exposure limit for noise is ninety decibels, as an eight-hour, time-weighted average. In the living room downstairs, it is at least a hundred-and-ten and no one should be exposed to that amount of noise for more than a minute and twenty-nine seconds without any form of protection. You should read the Labour Inspectorate home page."

I looked at my son. His ears were truly sensitive. Come to think of it, he had always been highly sensitive to loud sounds, and I wondered if it had any connection to the fact that he could hear the bats so well.

"You just gave me an idea," I said and got up. I walked across the street and knocked on Jack's door. He smiled when he opened the door.

"What a pleasant surprise."

I blushed. I knew he liked me and I liked him too. Then I remembered Morten and shook it off. I didn't want to complicate things.

"Hi. Listen, I know you have some hearing-protection, noise-canceling headphones lying around in your studio. I saw them the last time I was out there."

"Yeah, I use them when I sometimes work as a construction worker to earn a little extra money.

"Could I borrow them for my son?"

FORTY-SIX
MARCH 2013

The handsome husband had only shot him once. Thomas had been hit in the shoulder, but luckily, it was just a cut. No bullet had entered his body as he ran across the dirt roads and through the forest. Not that the handsome husband hadn't wanted to shoot him. He had fired several shots, but luckily for Thomas, he wasn't a very good shot. Some of the bullets had hit tree trunks next to him and most of them had ended up in the dirt behind him. Thomas had managed to jump into his car and drive off.

Now, a couple of weeks later, he was back, hiding outside of Ellen's house, watching her through the open window. She was getting ready to go out. She had a lunch date in town with an old girlfriend she hadn't seen in a long while. Ellen was whistling while putting on makeup. *Not that she ever needed it*, Thomas thought while studying her with a smile.

His shoulder hurt now and then, especially when he tried to move it, but not as much as his heart was hurting from her rejection.

How could you betray me like this, Ellen? How could you say those words when you know how deep our love is?

After the incident, Thomas had driven to the beach with the intent of killing himself. Just bringing an end to all of the suffering inside of him. He sat behind the wheel and cried for hours, hearing Ellen's harsh words in his head over and over again.

"I don't love you, Thomas. It's not real. It's all in your head. I love my husband. It's just an illusion."

How could you say those horrible things, Ellen? How could you hurt me so deeply? Me, who has loved you since the first time I ever laid eyes on you. Don't you know we're meant to be?

While sitting in his car on the beach, Thomas had realized he didn't want to kill himself. No, he wasn't the one who should be punished for this. He wasn't the bad guy. They were. They both were. Ellen and that husband of hers. Oh, how it enraged him to think about them. But mostly her. She was the one who had hurt him the most. She was the one who had said those horrible things to him.

So Thomas returned to doing what he had done for the last seven years nonstop. He resumed following Ellen wherever she went. In his anger, he dreamed about making her suffer the way he had suffered. He fantasized about kidnapping her and keeping her locked up somewhere. He could make her love him again. He knew he could. If not, then there was no way around it. If he couldn't have her, then no one should.

Ellen was humming as she got up from the makeup table. Her husband entered the bedroom and kissed her on the cheek. They laughed. Thomas felt his blood boil.

"I can't tell you how much freer I feel since you got rid of him, Mads. I am so grateful. I feel liberated after many years in captivity, constantly worrying about him and what he was going to come up with next. Now I can just live my life. I can go into town without constantly looking in my mirrors to see if he is following me. I don't have to fear walking the streets alone. I'm finally free."

"He will never bother you again," the husband said. "I promise you that much. He is out of here. I gave him a lesson he will never forget. You never have to worry about him again."

"Thank you so much, Mads," she said with a deep sigh. "I was against the use of force on him, but I'm beginning to think you were right. It's the only language that type of person understands."

The skin on Thomas's arm was crumbling. He felt like screaming, hearing them talk like this.

Calm down. You'll get your revenge. Don't you worry.

Thomas giggled and held a hand over his mouth so they wouldn't hear it. Then he heard the doorbell and opened his eyes wide.

Showtime.

He listened as Ellen walked toward the front door and opened it. Thomas heard Ellen scream and found it hard not to laugh.

"What's the matter, sweetie?" the husband yelled. Then Thomas heard the sound of his boots on the floor as he ran to the door to see why his wife was screaming. Thomas dared to lift his head enough to be able to see them through the open door. Ellen was standing in the doorway bent over the package that had been delivered to her. She was crying, holding a hand to her mouth.

You're a genius, Thomas. Sending them an empty coffin was brilliant.

He looked at Ellen who was holding his note in her hand. The note that said, between them, the so familiar words.

Till death parts us.

FORTY-SEVEN
NOVEMBER 2013

Lisa placed Per Egon's body in a small storeroom in the back of the library, then took the back door out. She ran with the stroller back to her house where she took a shower and washed the blood off of her hands, packed an overnight bag, and called Christian to tell him what was happening.

"Do you mean to tell me we're going to spend the night at some stranger's house?" Christian sighed.

"Well, the police seem to think we need the protection," Lisa said, while Margrethe was fussing on her hip. "I need to feed Margrethe soon. I really don't have time for this, Christian. Just grab Amalie and Jacob and bring them over there, will you?"

Christian sighed. He was probably rubbing his eyebrows like he always did when he was concerned or troubled.

"You really think that's a good idea? I have a game I wanted to watch tonight. I was really looking forward to it."

"Well, maybe you could skip that for once, huh? I mean your wife's life is in danger so maybe... just MAYBE you could skip one game, huh? You think?"

"All right, all right. Don't have a fit here. I'll be there, and I'll bring the kids."

Lisa hung up, then grabbed baby Margrethe and started feeding her a bottle. After half an hour, she packed her car with the baby and bags and drove off.

The woman named Emma lived close to the beach at a great location, worth a lot of money. The house was big, but very old. The garden hadn't been taken care of for ages and looked like one big mess. Lisa sighed and helped Margrethe out of her car seat. A police car was parked next to her. The two officers inside of it followed her with their eyes. One of them got out when she had finally gotten Margrethe out and grabbed one of the bags from the car.

"Lisa Rasmussen?" the officer said.

"Yes. I was told to come here and bring my family."

The officer lifted his cap and nodded. "Yes. We believe it's the safest thing for you. Officer Bredballe will arrive shortly as well and stay inside the house for the night to make sure everyone is safe."

Lisa tilted her head. "What a relief."

And could you please tell me who is going to save us from all the germs and viruses we're going to be infected with in this old, dirty house?

"Well, go on in. They're waiting for you inside."

Lisa smiled, then walked toward the stairs leading to the front door. Emma Frost opened the door when Lisa rang the doorbell.

"Welcome," she said with a smile. "I'm so glad you decided to come here. Let me grab that." Emma reached out for the bag, but Lisa held it close to her body.

"You don't need to," she said and walked past the plump woman. "Where can I put it?"

Emma walked up the stairs and showed Lisa into a room.

Lisa walked in and breathed a sigh of anxiety. It wasn't clean, there was a lot of dust in the corners and fingerprints on the walls. How was she supposed to sleep in here?

"Everything on the bed is clean. There are towels in the bathroom. I have another room ready next door for your older kids."

There was a lot of screaming coming from downstairs. Children laughing, yelling, running up the stairs and past the room. Lisa felt dizzy and sat down on a chair with the baby on her lap.

"Yeah. I'm sorry about that," Emma said with a grin.

What's there to laugh about, you fleshy monster with no self-control? Being chubby isn't cute, if that's what you think.

"It's kind of a madhouse today." Emma looked at Lisa. "Are you sure you don't need any help?"

"I have more bags in the car," Lisa groaned. "I need them."

"Just hand me the car keys, and I'll go get them," Emma said.

Lisa sat in the chair like she was frozen, making sure to not touch anything while Emma got her bags for her. When she handed back the car keys, Lisa pulled out a bottle of hand sanitizer and wiped them before she put them in her purse.

Emma stared at her, then smiled awkwardly. Maybe it was just the way she looked. There was something awkward about her, Lisa thought. Maybe it was just the fact that she was wearing a very dirty apron smeared in dough and she had flour in her hair.

"Let me know if there is anything else you need," Emma said.

Lisa shook her head. "I'm fine. Thank you."

"Okay. There will be freshly baked buns in fifteen minutes in the kitchen if you'd like to join us," Emma said with a horrendous smile on her chubby face. Lisa felt terrified to have to eat anything that woman had created.

Probably stuffed with carbs and butter. Terrifying. And germs. Oh, the horror.

As soon as Emma left, Lisa opened one of her bags. Bottles of cleaning products tumbled out on the floor.

FORTY-EIGHT
NOVEMBER 2013

The strange woman was cleaning her room. I could smell the cleaning products all the way into my bathroom where I had gone in to take a shower and wash off all the flour from baking. I could hear her scrub and splash water as I passed her door on my way down the stairs.

I chuckled, then walked into the kitchen where Sophia was still sitting sipping coffee while baby Alma was playing on the floor, trying to stand upright by holding on to the handles on the drawers. Maya had taken the rest of the children outside to play in the garden, so it was almost quiet inside the house.

"What's so funny?" Sophia asked, when she noticed my expression.

"That woman. That Lisa character. She brought her own cleaning products, and now she is up there scrubbing down the entire room."

Sophia laughed loudly. "Yes. That sure sounds like something she would do."

I took the buns out of the oven and called the kids. It felt like I was caught in a whirlwind. All five kids stormed into the kitchen and threw themselves at the buns, ate and drank their chocolate milk greedily, then stormed back out. Maya looked like she'd been in a tornado.

"Are you okay?" I asked. "Can you handle them?"

"Sure," she said with a smile. "But you owe me big time for this."

"I have a feeling I will pay for it one day," I said.

"Oh, you will," Maya said with a mischievous smile, then disappeared through the kitchen door.

"I owe her too, you know," Sophia said. "And you."

I buttered a bun and took a bite. "Nah. What are friends for? I'm just glad to help you."

"How's the book coming?"

"It's not," I said. "It's not coming at all. I need something good to happen soon. It can't just be a book about parents searching for their kids if they don't find them. I need a positive success story."

"It'll come. I'm sure you and Morten will be able to find one of these girls soon," Sophia said and finished her coffee.

Someone was at the door. I walked out to open it. A man with two children was standing outside.

"You must be Lisa's family," I said, and shook the husband's hand.

I showed them upstairs and helped them get settled in their rooms. The children wanted to play in the garden as well, so I showed them outside. A few minutes later, Lisa's husband, Christian, came down and asked if there was a TV somewhere that he could watch his game on. I helped him find his game on my TV, then walked back to the kitchen where Sophia helped me prepare dinner for the entire bunch.

A little after seven, all the children had eaten and we put them to bed so they were all asleep by eight. Lisa had hardly touched any of her dinner and seemed to be wiping everything with her sanitizer while her husband was yelling in the living room at his favorite soccer team.

Sophia and I sat in the living room for a couple of hours and talked after baby Alma had gone to sleep as well. Sophia seemed to have slightly forgotten the threat to her life, and she seemed much more relaxed and comfortable. We had a great evening and I enjoyed her company a lot, even if I was constantly looking at the clock, wondering what was holding Morten up, as he'd told me he would come over and spend the night to make sure we were safe. I had expected him for dinner, but all night, he hadn't even answered his phone. I was worried and a little anxious. It had been dark for several hours now and with all the big panoramic windows in my house, it felt like anyone could stand outside and look in. I didn't have curtains on all of them, but those that did, I closed to make sure the killer wasn't outside spying on all of us, waiting to make his move.

Finally, about nine-thirty, someone knocked on the door. I got up and walked out to open it while the rest of the people in the room watched me fearfully.

"Will you relax?" I said, before opening the door. "The killer probably won't knock on the door, now will he?"

Morten looked very serious when I opened the door and let him in. He walked straight to the living room. "You're all here. That's good," he said.

"What's going on?" Sophia asked nervously.

"There has been another one, right?" I asked.

Morten exhaled. "Two," he said.

The entire room gasped. Even Christian, whose game was finally over, turned off the TV.

"Two?" I asked. "How? Who?"

"Nora," he said with a heavy voice. "Nora was found sitting in a car downtown. The car was on fire. I guess the killer wised up about trying to drive her into the ocean. He probably knew we were observing the area, waiting for him to show up."

"Oh, my God!" I exclaimed.

"Yes. She is dead. The firefighters pulled her out of the car, but it was too late."

"That is terrible," Sophia said.

"Hardly a surprise," Lisa said.

I stared at her for a second, then decided to ignore her remark. "Who was the other?" I asked.

Morten looked at me. His eyes had grown so serious the last couple of days. This case was really getting to him. "Per Egon. The librarian."

"The guy who's running for city council?" Sophia asked. "Oh, my God. Why would the killer choose him?"

Morten shrugged. "Why would he kill anyone here? We have no idea of this killer's motive so far. We only know that all the women have been in the same mothers' group."

"Was it the same as the others?" I asked. "Was he bitten by animals and shot like the women were?"

"That's the tricky part. No he wasn't. He was found in a storeroom at the library, stabbed to death."

"So it could be someone else then?" I asked.

Morten shook his head. "I have no idea anymore. This case is so strange. No matter how hard I try, I can't connect the dots."

"Maybe you need some sleep," I said. "What do the investigators from Copenhagen say?"

"That it is very likely the same killer. This many killings at the same time in the same town is rarely coincidental. It has to be connected somehow."

"Maybe the librarian got in the way of the killer somehow?" Lisa suggested.

Morten looked at her and nodded. "Maybe," he said pensively. He looked at me. "Could I have a word with you in private?"

"Sure."

We apologized then walked into the kitchen where Morten

grabbed my face between his hands and kissed me. "Sorry," he said when he was done.

"Don't be. I'm not sorry."

"I just needed to kiss you; that was all."

I blushed. "It's okay."

"There is one thing I wanted to tell you that I couldn't say out there."

"And that is?"

"Lisa Rasmussen was seen at the library today. Per Egon's wife, who also works there, said she arrived earlier with her stroller and then left out the back door. She went to talk to Per Egon. Apparently, Lisa is the one who last saw him alive."

I felt like laughing but stopped myself. "Lisa? Do you really think she could have hurt him?"

"I don't know. But I have to look at the facts. The wife found him in the storeroom an hour after Lisa was there to talk to him."

"So you think Lisa is the killer?"

Morten shrugged. "She knew all the other victims. Plus, her house was the last one the plumber was supposed to visit."

"Wow," I said. "Shouldn't you arrest her or something?"

"I can't do anything right now. She needs to be taken to the station for questioning. I'll do that in the morning. Just because she was there right before the man was killed, doesn't mean she is the killer. I mean, how is she supposed to have planted Nora in the middle of town in a burning car when I assume she has been here all evening?"

"Yeah, she arrived about five o'clock."

"There you go. Unless she is really smart or maybe has someone helping her, she can't be the killer. It's not that easy."

"So what are you saying here?"

"I'm saying that, right now, it could be anyone. Including anyone in this house."

FORTY-NINE
NOVEMBER 2013

The atmosphere in the living room was tense when we returned from the kitchen. Sophia and Lisa had started to fight.

"What the hell is going on here?" I asked.

"Lisa is being obnoxious," Sophia said.

"We can't all be as common as you," Lisa said with a snort. "Some have to rise above the crowd and set new standards."

I looked at the two women, not understanding fully what was going on, but understanding enough to know that this was going to be a long night. I, for one, wasn't going to go to bed. Not after what Morten had told me. If Lisa turned out to be the killer, I was going to keep a close eye on her all night.

"Now let's all sit down for a little while and calm down," I said with the same authority I used to split up my kids when they were fighting. Lisa and Sophia obeyed. I sat down on a chair in the corner while Morten lit a fire in the fireplace. No one spoke for at least twenty minutes. It felt awkward and a little horrifying. I kept staring at Lisa wondering how she had done it. How could she kidnap her friends and kill them by shooting them? Then I looked at her husband, wondering if he was her accomplice. Was he the one who had taken care of

Nora while Lisa came to my house to excessively clean it? Was he the strength behind this while she was the brains?

"Anyone care for a glass of sherry?" Christian asked, all of a sudden. "I brought some just in case we needed it. And I do have a feeling we need it now."

Christian pulled out his briefcase from the hallway and opened it. He showed us the bottle with a grin. "This should make the evening more bearable."

Sophia got up and found glasses for all of us in the kitchen. Christian poured some in them and Sophia handed the glasses out.

"I really shouldn't," I said.

"Don't be boring, Emma," Sophia said. "You need it as much as any of us."

I took the glass and stared into it wondering if they had drugged it. Then I watched Christian lift his, toast, and guzzle it down.

"Give me one of those," Lisa said, and grabbed a glass out of Sophia's hand. Then she drank it greedily.

If they can do it... I thought and lifted the glass and sipped from it. Sophia drank hers as well while Christian poured himself another one. Morten didn't touch his and left it on the table. The alcohol warmed my stomach and made me calmer. Sophia handed me another and had one more herself. She had stopped breastfeeding just a few days ago, and I guessed she was enjoying the fact that she could have a couple of drinks now. I drank one more, then told them I had enough. The alcohol made me dizzy, but very, very relaxed. Morten seemed troubled. I felt like hugging him and letting him know how much I liked him. Christian and Lisa were drinking heavily now. They were laughing and pouring more into their glasses. I couldn't help staring at them, wondering how many they had killed. Imagining how and where they had done it and wondering if they were planning on attacking us while we were asleep.

Freaking Bonnie and Clyde in my own house.

I looked at the half-empty bottle of sherry on the table. Maybe that was why Christian had taken out the bottle? It wasn't that it was drugged. No, it was just to make us fall asleep, wasn't it? Were they going to kill all of us? Or just some? Would they kill one then come back for more? Would they hurt the kids?

The thoughts made me clench my fists. I decided I wasn't going to let them do anything to anyone. I was going to stay awake all night and keep both my eyes and ears open. Nothing was going to get past me.

If they planned anything this night, then they'd have to deal with me first. Well, me and hopefully Morten.

FIFTY
MARCH 2013

They tried going to the police, but no one believed them. Thomas watched through a window when they showed an officer the note and the coffin, but he told them Thomas was dead and he even had a death certificate to prove it.

It had to be someone else. Maybe it was just a joke.

Ellen and her handsome husband left the police station in Nordby while Thomas followed them. He jumped inside his car and followed them down the road, leaving a couple of cars between them in order to not be seen. He had become an expert at remaining hidden.

From afar, he could tell they were fighting in the car. The handsome husband was yelling and gesticulating heavily while Ellen only got a word in here and there. They continued like that until they reached the shopping district downtown, and the husband stopped the car in front of the liquor shop. Thomas could tell Ellen didn't want him to go in there. She pulled his shirt and appeared agitated. Thomas drove past her car and parked down a side street, where he was able to stay hidden and still see when the husband came out of the shop.

A minivan drove up on his side and stopped for a red light.

Thomas turned and looked inside. In it, he spotted five women. They seemed to be arguing as well. The lady driving was yelling and screaming at the ones in the back seat. Thomas stopped looking at them and turned his head to look at Ellen again, when he realized she had decided to get out of the car.

Where are you going?

Next to Thomas's car was a bakery. Was she heading for the bakery? She did have a bad habit of overeating when she was upset. Something that had started to show on her hips.

You know you'll regret it.

That was when it dawned on Thomas. This was it. This was his moment. It would be the easiest thing in the world. He could walk right up to her and grab her before anyone saw it and put her in his car. It would be a piece of cake. He could pretend he had a weapon, a gun in his pocket, and she would follow him without a word.

Yes, yes. That is it. It's now or never, Thomas. This is your moment to shine.

Thomas felt exhilarated. He clapped his hands and looked at Ellen as she walked across the street. Thomas exited his car as well and started walking toward her. She was crossing the road. A sound startled Thomas, and he turned just in time to see the minivan miss him. He looked in the van in the split second it drove past him and noticed the woman driver was still yelling at the women in the back and not watching the road at all. Panic hit him and his heart stopped.

Ellen!

Tires screeched, then a thud followed and everything went quiet inside of Thomas. He saw people staring at the minivan with open mouths, while others covered their eyes with their hands. The minivan finally stopped farther down the road, and all the women got out of the car. One of them kneeled on the ground and threw up. Another stood with her mouth open like she was screaming but Thomas couldn't hear her. He heard nothing, not even the handsome husband's screams when he came running out of the liquor shop to throw himself at Ellen's dead body on the asphalt.

Thomas didn't even hear the sirens when the ambulance and police arrived and cleared the street. He stared at the ground where the remains of Ellen were scattered all over the street. The last thing Thomas remembered was when his eyes, for a split second, met those of the handsome husband who was crying helplessly while the paramedics tried to help him get away from his dead wife.

FIFTY-ONE
NOVEMBER 2013

Thomas was looking in the windows of the pretty woman's house. She wasn't beautiful like Ellen had been, but he thought she was pretty, in a casual sort of way. Emma was her name, he had learned. And she was harboring the two women who Thomas was looking for.

The last two from the car that hit Ellen.

They thought they could hide, didn't they? But they didn't know Thomas very well. They didn't know he knew everything about them, every friend they had, every move they had made the past eight months. He had followed them, all of them, written down their routines in detail, making sure he never left anything out. He knew when Lisa had a doctor's appointment and when Sophia was getting her alimony check because then she would go shopping for new clothes for her many children. He had kept track of all five of them to make his revenge perfect.

After the accident, the handsome husband left the farm outside of town... abandoned it. Thomas couldn't just leave everything the way the husband had done. He kept coming back, remembering Ellen and not wanting to let her go. Even if the house was now empty except for a few pieces of furniture and other things they had left behind... among them all of Ellen's clothes, which Thomas smelled every day and even wore on some days when he really missed her and thought he wasn't going to survive without her.

For weeks, he cried every day while sitting in her bedroom with the windows closed so her scent wouldn't disappear. One day, there had been someone in there with him. He had heard a strange sound, then walked to the kitchen to discover a small bat on the floor. It was trying to fly, but it had broken its wing. Seeing himself a little in the young bat with a broken wing, Thomas picked it up and in the following days he nursed it back to health. Soon, he found another one hanging under the ceiling. As he walked around the house, he realized it wasn't alone. So he built them a cage and put them in it. For quite a while, they were his only company.

It was one day while feeding them, by letting them suck his blood through an open wound, that he came up with the idea for his revenge. He wanted so badly to punish someone for Ellen's death, and who better than those crazy women? He knew it was all their fault. Especially the driver. She hadn't been paying any attention, she hadn't kept her eyes on the road as she was supposed to.

As the days passed in the empty house, Thomas became more and more convinced that it was the women's fault and he started planning his revenge. He started following each one of them, and soon, he was very busy keeping track of everything they did and who they did it with.

Now eight months later, he had killed three of them by shooting them with the handsome man's old rifle that he had left behind.

Thomas felt better each time he killed one of these despicable women. What bothered him the most was that woman, Lisa. He recognized her as the woman he had been watching for a short while after Ellen had moved to the countryside. There wasn't a day when he didn't regret not having killed her back then. The thought came again and again like a thief at night.

If only I had... No, no. You mustn't punish yourself for what happened to Ellen. It wasn't your fault. It was theirs. It was especially hers.

Lisa Rasmussen was a terrible woman, Thomas had come to know. He was the one who had handed the papers to her opponent, Per Egon, the ones showing that Lisa never took her exam. An idiot like Per Egon never would have thought of this himself. So, Thomas helped him a little. But Thomas had seen Lisa do horrible things to people. Oh, boy. He had even seen her punch a small boy in the gut and knock the air out of him, just because he cut in line in the sweets shop while the owner looked away. Entering the shop just as she did it, Thomas heard the boy start to cry. Lisa then whispered in the boy's ear that she would kill his dog if he ever told anyone. So he didn't.

No, there was no doubt that Thomas was doing the world a huge favor by getting rid of her and the same probably went for the rest of the women. They were all horrible creatures.

Three down, two to go.

Thomas giggled as he watched all of them gathered in the living room. All he had to do now was to make his pick. Who would go first?

FIFTY-TWO
NOVEMBER 2013

By one o'clock, we all slept heavily. I fought the urge to fall asleep for as long as I could, but soon I dozed off as well. Dizzy from the sherry and exhausted from all the agitation, I closed my eyes for just one second and then fell into a deep sleep on my couch. I thought Morten would hold out, but when I opened my eyes and realized it was light out, the first thing I saw was him sitting in the chair with his head tilted backward, sound asleep. The rest of the company had disappeared.

"Morten," I whispered.

He grunted. "Not now."

"Morten. Wake up."

"What?"

"Wake up. We fell asleep. It's morning."

Morten sat up with a startled look. "We fell asleep?"

"I'm afraid so."

"I'm so sorry, Emma. I was supposed to stay awake."

"I'll go check on everyone upstairs," I said, and got up. I hurried into Maya's room and found her in a deep sleep snuggled up in the middle of the bed, drooling on her pillow. I smiled and backed out of the room quietly. Then I entered

Victor's room. He was already awake, sitting in his chair with his notebook on his knees, writing in it while rocking back and forth.

"Hi, buddy. Did you sleep well?" I asked. Then I realized he was still wearing the headphones I borrowed from Jack. I approached him and kneeled in front of him. His face seemed tormented. I grabbed one of the ears on the headphones and pulled it off of him.

"Hi, sweetie. Did you sleep okay?"

Victor lifted his eyes and looked into mine. It was always so intense when he did that. My heart rate went up.

"Is something wrong?"

"The bats are screaming, Mommy."

My heart was beating faster now. "Is someone with them now, Victor?"

Victor removed my hand from the headphones, then pressed it closer to his ears like they weren't enough to keep out the sound. Then he nodded. I was struck by a sudden feeling, rose to my feet, and stormed toward Sophia's room. I opened the door and found the bed empty. I gasped, then walked inside.

"Sophia?" I called out.

Baby Alma was babbling from her travel bed in the corner. I walked to her and picked her up. "Where is Mommy, Alma?"

I looked at the bed. It hadn't been slept in at all. I walked into the bathroom with a pounding heart. "Sophia?" I called again and again. But no answer came. I found her clothes on the chair so she had undressed and gotten ready for bed, but then what? Where did she go after that?

Sophia would never, ever leave Alma.

The thought made me run down the hallway while calling Sophia's name and looking into all of the rooms, one after another. I wondered if she had gone in to sleep with her other children and found their room. They were all awake; three of them were fighting and throwing pillows. One was sitting on the floor crying, while the oldest was trying to comfort him. They all froze as I entered the room.

"Have any of you seen your mother?" I asked, trying not to sound worried. "Alma needs to be fed."

"There is milk in the refrigerator," the oldest, Christoffer, said.

"Has your mother been in here this morning?" I asked.

Christoffer looked concerned. "No. Why?"

I shook my head and forced a smile. "No reason. I'm just looking for her, that's all."

The twins Anne and Derik looked at me with big eyes. "You can't find Mommy?" they asked in unison.

"No, no. I'm sure she is downstairs. It's just a big house."

The two oldest, Christoffer and Ida, knew I was lying. I could tell by the worry that was suddenly planted across their faces. "I'll find her," I said. "Just take care of one another, will you?"

They promised and I closed the door. I ran from door to door, knocking, then went back to Maya's room and woke her up.

"Please take care of Alma. Sophia is missing. I need to find her. There is milk in the refrigerator."

FIFTY-THREE
NOVEMBER 2013

They were fighting again. They had been going at it all morning and none of them remembered why anymore. Lisa sighed and looked at Amalie and Jacob who were yelling at each other, one screaming louder than the other while baby Margrethe was crying loudly, like she was trying to drown out all of them. This was, all of a sudden, a very small room. The kids had come in to get their clothes and use the bathroom.

"Mom, Amalie called me stupid," Jacob said.

"No, I did not. I never said that," Amalie whined.

"You're stupid," Jacob said.

"Moooom!"

"Can't you just take your clothes and go dress in your own room?" Christian asked with a groan. He hadn't even gotten out of bed yet. It was, after all, Sunday. That was his excuse.

Lisa rubbed her eyes. She was trying to get Margrethe to take the bottle, but she refused. If she was crying because she was hungry, then why wouldn't she eat?

"Moooom!" Amalie yelled again. "Aren't you going to say anything to him?"

Lisa exhaled and looked at her oldest.

"That is so typical," Amalie said, stomping her feet on the floor. "You always take his side. You never hear what I'm saying. You never listen to me. Never!"

Lisa looked at her husband for help, but he had closed his eyes and pulled the covers over his head to shut them all out. Lisa groaned while trying to stuff the bottle into Margrethe's small mouth. She spat it out, then cried even louder. Lisa closed her eyes to calm herself down. Amalie reached her hand out and whacked her brother on the head. Jacob cried out.

"Moooom! Amalie hit me."

Come on, take the bottle. Forget about everybody else, sweetheart, just take the bottle and you'll feel much better. Please stop crying, would you? Please? I need you to stop, sweetie.

"Moooom?" Jacob said again. Then he reached over and pulled Amalie's hair till she screamed.

"Moooom!"

Lisa didn't want to lift her head and look at them. She tried hard to focus on her baby and get her to eat. The crying increased and Margrethe was getting red in the face. Christian moaned from the bed. Jacob and Amalie screamed and pulled each other's hair.

Just try to stay calm. Think of a meadow. Think of the ocean, the beach, the forest, anything calm and quiet. Count backward from a hundred. Picture a field of flowers and you lying in it staring at the blue sky above with nothing to worry about. Just stay calm. Whatever you do just stay calm, for Pete's sake!

"Moooom?" Amalie said, crying.

"Moooom?" Jacob said, crying even louder, holding a hand to his head where Amalie had hit him.

"Lisa?" Christian said. "Could you please get them to be quiet? I need my sleep. I drank too much of that sherry last night. Do you have any aspirin? Lisa?"

Lisa stared at the baby who still refused to take the bottle. Her body was shaking as she tried to stay calm and counted.

"Eighty-nine, eighty-eight," she said, while closing her eyes. But the pictures inside of her head were no longer of a beautiful meadow or a quiet forest; no, they were of blood. Blood rushing out of Christian's body after she had stabbed him with the carving fork she was still carrying in her purse, still smeared with Per Egon's blood from yesterday. No matter how hard she tried, she couldn't get the picture to go away and replace it with something soothing and calming instead.

"Lisa?" Christian repeated.

"Mom?" the kids both said.

She opened her eyes and looked at them, but saw nothing but a river of blood running toward her and their faces torn in distress and pain.

"WHAT?" she yelled.

There was a knock on the door and they all went quiet. The knocking intensified, then she heard Emma's voice on the other side. "Lisa? I know you're in there, please open the door."

Lisa handed Christian the baby and the bottle. "Here, you try now." He looked baffled, and opened his mouth to complain, but a look from Lisa made him stop. She opened the door.

"What?"

Emma looked furious. She was out of breath as she spoke. "What have you done to her?"

"Done to whom?" Lisa asked.

"Sophia. Where is she?"

Lisa shook her head to make sure this wasn't some stupid dream. "How should I know?"

"I think you did something to her. She is missing. I can't find her anywhere."

"I beg your pardon? Is that any way to treat a guest in your house?" Lisa asked.

The ugly Officer Bredballe came running up the stairs, panting. He stood behind Emma. "She's nowhere downstairs, or in the garden."

"That leads us back to you, Lisa," Emma said. "I know you've done something to her. I want to know what you did to Sophia. Where is she?"

"This is getting really old," Lisa said. "I haven't done anything to Sophia. Now, if you'll excuse me, I have a minor family crisis I have to attend to," she said and turned to look at her family. They were all staring back at her. Except the baby, who had finally accepted the bottle.

"Is this true, Lisa? Have you done something to Sophia?" Christian asked.

"Mom?" Amalie asked with an accusing voice.

Jacob didn't say anything. He stared at his mother with distrust. "Are you kidding me?" Lisa asked while the fury threatened to explode inside of her. "Are you freaking kidding me here?"

No one in the room spoke for quite a while. Officer Bredballe broke the silence. "Let's not jump to conclusions here."

Not knowing what else to do, Lisa took one last look at her husband, then reached for her purse on the table, grabbed it, and stormed out the room knocking over Emma Frost on her way out and making her fall into the arms of Officer Bredballe. The two of them tumbled to the floor and once they were back up, Lisa was long gone.

FIFTY-FOUR
NOVEMBER 2013

I called my dad and asked him to come over and help Maya look after Sophia's kids. He came a few minutes later. I went into Victor's room and pulled off his headphones.

"You're coming with me."

Downstairs, Morten was already calling the station. On his way out the door, he turned and kissed me. "We'll comb the entire island to find Lisa," he said. "We'll find her. She can't go far."

"No, but she might kill Sophia if you don't catch her," I yelled after him as he sprang toward his car.

I looked at Victor who was standing next to me. "Come on, buddy. Let's go."

We walked to my car and drove off. "I need your help with this, Vic," I said as soon as we had left our street. "I believe you can hear those bats, and I believe you're hearing them right now, am I right?"

He didn't answer but he didn't protest either. "I'll take that as a yes."

"I know it's a long shot, but I believe Sophia is with those bats, and I believe you can lead us to them if you follow the sound. Do you think you can do that? Do you think you can lead me there?"

I turned my head and looked at Victor for some sort of signal that he understood what I was asking him to do. Then he nodded.

"Great. Tell me where to go."

We drove around in the neighborhood for quite a while. I was beginning to lose hope that he'd be able to help me with this, when Victor finally said something.

"Turn right here."

"Are you hearing them now?" I asked.

He didn't answer. Probably thought it was needless. "And now left."

Then he went quiet for a long time and I kept driving, thinking it was odd that we had to go this far away. When we passed the city limit sign I became concerned. "Are you sure about this, buddy? We're outside of town now."

He remained quiet. I chose to trust him. After all, he was my only hope now. I looked at my phone to see if Morten had called or texted, but there was nothing. I felt so furious inside that I had let Lisa right into my home like this. She had to be behind it somehow. I just couldn't figure out how. As the landscape changed, I wondered how on earth Lisa would even be able to do this, to kidnap Sophia or any of the others. Her husband didn't seem to be in on it, after all. And, she had a baby.

I shook my head. No it was her. I was certain it was. It had to be. It fit so well. She knew all of the victims, plus she was seen at the library yesterday. Plus I had seen something in her this morning when she opened the door to her room. Some kind of uncontrollable anger that I remember having seen in the eyes of Officer Dan when I had just moved here and he tried to kill me and my family. It was in Lisa's eyes as well. A hurt combined with rage. It was in her eyes and had convinced me she was capable of doing this. Of doing things this cruel. Wasn't she?

"Turn left," Victor suddenly said very loudly.

"But, Victor, there isn't anything here. Nothing but a dirt road leading to some old farm."

Victor was rocking back and forth now in his seat, holding his hands to his ears. He seemed in distress, in pain even.

"Is it very loud now, Victor?" I asked.

"They're screaming, Mommy."

"You don't need to say any more," I said and turned up the dirt road. On a mailbox by the road it read *Ellen and Mads Andersen*.

FIFTY-FIVE
NOVEMBER 2013

Lisa was punching the steering wheel of her car as she drove across town. Tears of wrath were rolling across her cheeks.

Who the hell does she think she is? Talking to me like that? Someone should teach that woman a lesson. Teach her how to behave toward guests. I have never... how dare she be so rude!

Lisa wiped a tear off her cheek and realized she was driving in circles. She had no idea where to go. She couldn't go home, because they would probably look for her there. She couldn't go back to her family, because they all thought she was a vicious killer. It hurt her so deeply that they would think that about her. Yes, she had a temper, and, yes, she couldn't always control it, but the people she killed had deserved it. They had it coming, and she was doing everybody a favor by removing them. She didn't kill Simone Beaumont, who had, in fact, been Lisa's friend and the one she liked best in the group. Didn't they see her tears when she received the news that she was dead? Didn't they feel her pain? She was sincerely upset when it happened. Didn't they know that? Okay, so she had fantasized about hurting Sophia now and then, especially because she was the one spilling coffee all over her car right before the accident, right before they hit that woman in the street and killed her with the minivan. But she hadn't done anything about it. She really didn't plan to either. And whatever happened, Lisa certainly didn't deserve to be treated like that.

Like a common criminal.

Lisa stopped the car in a parking spot, then got out and started walking up the street. She was really hungry and needed something to eat and drink. Preferably a smoothie or something organic. She walked toward the Café Mimosa, where the faces were always smiling and the service impeccable. She pushed the door open and entered. The waitress named Julia smiled.

"Hi, Lisa," she said. "You're early today. Grab a table and I'll be right with you."

Lisa took in a deep breath and smiled back. She really needed Julia's friendly smile today. She decided to sit in the back so no one would see her from the street. Julia came out, still smiling. It brought tears to Lisa's eyes.

"So what can I bring you today, Lisa?" Julia said and looked around. "Where is the baby today? Are the rest of your group coming as well?"

Lisa sniffled. "It's just gonna be me today."

"Well, that's okay. Nice to have a couple of hours to yourself, huh? So what will it be? Do you need a few minutes to check the menu?"

Lisa shook her head. "No. I know what I want."

"The usual?" Julia asked. "Salad and a smoothie?"

Lisa opened her mouth to say yes, but hesitated. "You know what? Maybe I should try something new for once."

"Sure?"

"Give me a burger. The biggest you have. And put cheese on it. And fries. Oil-dripping fries. And bring me a Coke with that. Regular Coke with sugar. After that, I'll have a banana split with loads of chocolate sauce. Please make sure none of it is organic or gluten free, would you?"

Julia stared at Lisa like she had just fallen from the moon. Then she shook her head. "Sure. If that's what you want."

"It is. Thank you."

"No problem."

Julia left and Lisa stared at her own face in the mirrors that were covering the walls. It had been awhile since she last saw herself properly without the fake election smile. She had gotten old.

Well, so what? I'm forty-three and have a young baby. I'm entitled to look old. I'm entitled to eat a cheeseburger every now and then if I want to.

When the food arrived, Lisa ate greedily. Never had a meal tasted this good. She stuffed her face with fries and could hardly close her mouth to chew. Other customers arrived and stared at her while she was eating with her fingers, licking the grease off of them, and washing it all down with a Coke. She didn't care that they looked. For once in her life, she didn't care what anyone thought of her. She stuck her tongue out at them and laughed. Never had she felt this free.

It wasn't until halfway through the banana split, which she ate with her fingers, that she realized it wasn't only the other customers who were staring at her. So was the strange man she had seen at the café before. He was sitting at a table next to hers, giggling. As she looked into his eyes, she realized she had seen him once before. Eight months ago. When he got up and walked to her table, she remembered how her eyes had met his right before she took that fatal turn while yelling at Sophia, driving straight into that woman.

"Hello, Lisa," he said and sat in the chair across from her. "Finally we meet face to face."

FIFTY-SIX
NOVEMBER 2013

I knew we were going in the right direction just by looking at Victor. He was in more and more distress the closer we got to the house. I parked the car in front of the house and asked him to stay inside of it. The house looked empty. I knocked on the front door and when no answer came I walked inside. Most of the rooms were empty except for an old bedroom where I found women's clothes spread all over the floor. It smelled horrible and stuffy in there, like the windows hadn't been opened for months.

On the walls I found clippings from old newspapers taped to the walls. All were articles about some crash in downtown Nordby where a woman had been killed. I remembered the accident because Sophia had been in the car when it happened. She had told me all about it and had a hard time moving on. Her entire mothers' group had been in the minivan with all of their newborn babies. Lisa had been the driver.

The many articles told me I had to be in the right place. But they didn't explain why Lisa wanted to kill the rest of the group.

"Sophia?" I called out.

No answer. I walked to the kitchen, then another bedroom,

through what was supposed to be the living room but now was nothing but a big empty room with dust and dirt on the wooden planks.

"Sophia?"

I walked outside on the gravel and looked at Victor in the car. He was pressing his hands hard to cover his ears. I tried to listen but couldn't hear anything. Then I looked at his face. He was staring at the garage next to the house with anxious eyes.

"Sophia!" I said and stormed toward the door. It was locked. I tried to open it, but couldn't.

I put my ear on it to listen, then heard a squeaking. It sounded like an animal. "The bats!" I turned and looked at Victor. "The bats are in here, aren't they?"

I knocked on the garage door. "Sophia, are you in there? I'll come for you. I'll come and get you!"

"Emma?" a voice yelled back.

My heart skipped a beat. "Sophia? Are you in there?"

"Yes," she cried. "Yes. Please, help me get out. The bats are biting me."

"I'll be right there."

I stared at the door and wondered if there was another way in. I walked around the building. It wasn't an ordinary garage. It was bigger. Probably built for tractors. It seemed big enough. I walked to the back of it and found a back entrance. I pulled the handle, but it was locked. I hit it and kicked it till my eyes saw spots. Sophia was screaming inside.

"Get away from me, you monsters!"

I kicked the door again and this time it gave in. Some of the wood scattered and I could look inside the garage. I kicked it again and soon the hole was big enough for me to pass through.

"Sophia!" I said. I found a light switch by the door and flipped it. I gasped. Sophia was lying on the floor of a big cage packed with bats. They screamed as the light went on and moved to the roof of the cage. The skin on Sophia's back was swollen and covered with red marks. I found the key to the lock hanging on a nail right next to the door and opened it. Sophia crawled out, still holding her hands above her head to protect herself. I closed the door in a hurry as soon as she was out.

"Thank God," she moaned. "I really hate bats."

The bats were flapping their wings and squealing like they were very dissatisfied with me taking Sophia away. I kneeled next to her and hugged her.

"Careful. I'm kind of hurting here," she said.

"I'm sorry. I'm just so happy to have found you. Who did this to you? Did you see who it was?"

"I woke up in the cage. The last thing I remember was going outside last night before going to bed. I wanted to have a cigarette. Drinking alcohol always makes me long for a cigarette. So, I figured it would do no harm to grab one outside on your porch. But when I was about to light it, I was knocked out. I still have a huge bump right here to prove it. I think it was a baseball bat or something. It hurt like hell. Still does."

"We need to get you to a hospital right away."

"I'm not going anywhere. Except home to be with my children. Are they all right? Is Alma okay?"

"They're fine. They're with my dad and Maya."

"Lisa," Sophia suddenly exclaimed.

"What about her? Did she do this to you? Did she somehow put you in there?"

Sophia looked at me like I had finally lost it. "What are you talking about? It was a man who put me in that cage. A man who told me he was going to kill me like he'd killed the others. Then he told me why."

"The accident," I said.

"Yes. How did you know?"

"There were a bunch of articles about it in the bedroom. Is he her husband?"

"That's what I thought when he started talking about it, but then he told me they used to live here. The woman and her husband. Apparently he loved her, but wasn't married to her. He kept saying he was watching over her or something. He told me he had followed us ever since the accident that killed his beloved and that he was killing us because we had been careless. Lisa was driving the car, so he is mostly angry with her and that's why he's gone to get her now. He told me he wanted to kill us both at the same time. Just for the fun of it. Then he asked me if I was a good runner. I told him no and asked why. He said the weirdest thing. He said that whoever ran the fastest had the best chance of surviving. Anyway he was going to get her now, he told me. We must hurry."

FIFTY-SEVEN
NOVEMBER 2013

"So, Lisa. How do you want to do this?" the strange man with the very blue eyes asked. Lisa stared at him, wondering what he really wanted. Then she licked her fingers one by one to get the chocolate off.

"I have Sophia," he whispered.

Lisa didn't look at him. She kept licking her fingers like he wasn't there.

"I killed Susanne. And Nora."

Lisa chuckled. "Susanne isn't dead. And Nora was a cheating bitch."

"I killed Simone too. I know you cared about her, didn't you?" The man asked.

Lisa stopped licking and glanced at the man. He was smiling widely. Lisa knew that look. He was enjoying this. He wanted her to be afraid of him.

"What do you want?" she asked.

"I want you. You drove the car that day. You killed someone very dear to me."

"You're not her husband. Her husband left with the kids after the accident. They moved to the mainland," Lisa said.

"I'm not her husband. But I loved her. I loved her more than anything in this world. And you took her away from me. Just because you couldn't keep your eyes on the ROAD." The man said the last word while slamming his fist on the table. The other guests in the café turned to look at them.

"What are you staring at?" he asked them. That made them turn away. Lisa chuckled. She kind of liked the guy.

"So you want to kill me because I hit someone you loved with my car. Kind of lame, don't you think? A little cliché? I mean if you want to kill, then kill for a proper reason, have a cause, for crying out loud."

The man stared at her with a frown. "You listen to me, little missy. In my pocket, I have a gun. And I'm not afraid to use it. You come with me in my car now or I will kill you here if I have to."

Lisa wrinkled her forehead. Then she burst into laughter. "Good one."

"What?" The man seemed perplexed. "You don't believe me? Well, see for yourself," he said and pulled the gun out of his pocket.

"A gun!" someone said. Panic spread fast and the other customers screamed and soon the café was empty except for Lisa and the man.

"Oh my," Lisa said with a wide smile. "You certainly are a big, bad boy, aren't you?"

The man exhaled, then cocked the gun. "Don't make me do it," he said. "I just bought this gun from some guy who sold it to me from the back of his car. I paid a lot of money for it. And I really don't want to have to throw it in the ocean because it's considered evidence. Not now when I just got it."

Lisa chuckled again. She picked up the spoon and ate more of her banana split. People had started gathering outside the window now. People were yelling; some dared to peek in. Lisa really couldn't care less, but the commotion seemed to make the man a little nervous.

"Lisa. I'm asking you this one last time. Get up from your chair and walk with me through the back entrance. Now. Or I will shoot you."

"What's your name?"

"What?"

"I asked you politely what your name was. You don't answer with what. You're supposed to say excuse me or pardon me. Didn't your mother teach you any manners?"

"God, I hate you," he said, clenching his jaw.

"Well, the feeling is mutual. You still haven't answered me though. What is your name?"

"Thomas. My name is Thomas Hamilton. Remember it. Remember me. I will be the last person you see."

"Well, you and Sophia, I guess."

"What?"

"You just told me you had her. You used present tense. I have her, you said. That indicates she is still alive."

Lisa followed her last remark with her famous election smile, when Thomas reached over and slammed the gun's handle into her face, knocking her to the floor. It hurt like hell, and Lisa fought for a while to not sink out of consciousness. Thinking she was out cold, Thomas rose and stared at the crowd that had gathered outside. Meanwhile, Lisa managed to grab her purse and pull out the carving fork. When Thomas turned to look at her, she rose to her feet and planted the fork in his chest digging it deep until she felt it hit something vital, then she pressed it farther in. Thomas gasped and stared at her with wide-open eyes.

"What the... ?" The gun fell out of his hand and landed on the ground. Thomas's body fell to the floor. Lisa picked up the gun and put it on the table. Then she approached Thomas and pulled out the carving fork from his chest, while closing her eyes and enjoying the sound of it going through his flesh once again. Once it was out, she stabbed it into his abdomen, then pulled it out and stabbed it into his throat.

FIFTY-EIGHT
NOVEMBER 2013

I called Morten from my car as we raced toward town. Sophia was moaning in pain from the back seat, while Victor had finally found rest and told me the bats had stopped screaming.

"Emma?" Morten said. "Are you all right?"

"I have Sophia. She's all right but she needs medical attention. Did you find Lisa?"

"We just received a call from someone downtown telling us there is a commotion at Café Mimosa involving that lady from the election poster. I'm on my way down there," he said.

I looked at Sophia. "So are we. Listen. Lisa wasn't the one who took Sophia or killed any of the others in the mothers' group. It was a man. He's after Lisa right now."

"Got it," Morten said and hung up.

I took a shortcut and knew I could make it there faster. Five minutes later, I parked the car in the street in front of the café where a big crowd of people had gathered. I stormed toward it and elbowed my way through.

"I can't believe what she did; if I hadn't seen it with my own eyes, I wouldn't have believed it," someone mumbled.

"And he even had a gun," another said.

"She is one tough woman."

"You can say that again. I'm definitely voting for her. She is exactly what this town needs."

I reached the entrance and peeked in through the window. Julia the waitress was next to me, crying. "What happened?" I asked.

"He had a gun. He threatened her. But she took him down. Emma... it was... she was amazing. I can't believe it. He could have shot all of us, but she prevented it. She stopped him."

I turned my head and saw Lisa sitting inside the café at a table finishing what looked like a banana split while a man was lying on the floor in a pool of blood.

"People, people, please clear the street! Make room for the ambulance to come through." I recognized Morten's voice and turned to look at him while people started walking away.

"Are you okay?" he asked.

I nodded.

"What the hell happened?"

I shrugged. "I guess Lisa saved the day."

Another officer approached him from behind. "Someone just told me she stabbed him with a carving fork when he threatened to kill her."

"A carving fork?" Morten asked.

The officer shrugged. "Apparently so."

"Take all the statements you can. We'll leave the scene to the forensic team," Morten said.

"Lisa is a hero?" I asked.

"I guess so."

Lisa licked the spoon clean, then finished her soda and got up from her chair. Slowly, she walked outside. The crowd gasped, then spontaneously started clapping and cheering for her.

"Lisa for city council!" Someone standing close to me yelled.

"Lisa for prime minister," someone else yelled.

"Lisa. Lisa. Lisa." Others followed.

Lisa smiled the same way I had seen her do on the posters, then lifted her bloody hand and waved to the people the same way the royals waved. After she had taken in the applause, she walked toward me. She looked me in the eyes, then spoke. "It's quite a mess. Someone might want to clean that up."

EPILOGUE

A week later, Lisa Rasmussen was elected to the city council with more votes than any previous member. In her thank you speech on the local TV station, Lisa proclaimed that she was there to clean up the mess and that everybody could expect big changes in the town from now on.

I turned off the TV and looked at Morten sitting next to me. Then we both chuckled. We were planning a new trip, to Greece this time where one of the missing girls, Tenna, had miraculously turned up. She knocked on the door of a shelter one night and asked them to call the police. After sixteen years in captivity, she had finally managed to escape her captors. She didn't even know what country she was in, because she had been sold so many times and hadn't seen much except the inside of brothels. Now her family had been informed and was going to go down there and take her home. Morten and I were going with them. It was the perfect ending for my book and a new beginning for the broken family.

"So what do you say we take a couple of days off in Athens afterward?" Morten asked.

"That sounds really great. Play tourists a little while we're there?"

"That's what I thought. And maybe I'll get to see you naked without your skin being all blue," he said with a mischievous smile.

I gave him an elbow. "You wish," I said laughing.

"That is my wish."

"So the case is all closed now, huh?" I asked, to get another topic other than my nakedness on the table. I was planning on writing the book about Thomas and the killings of young mothers afterward.

"Yup. Thomas Hamilton killed Simone Beaumont and Nora Willumsen and tried to kill Susanne Arnholm and our friend Sophia before he met his match in Lisa Rasmussen."

"I am so glad Susanne at least survived and will be home with her children soon. That is a big relief, but what about the others? The plumber and the librarian? What happened to them?" I asked, and grabbed the last Ferrero Rocher in the package on the coffee table.

"Well, only one body, the librarian, has been found so far, and he was stabbed to death. It wasn't the same modus operandi, the same method as the rest. We suspect his wife did it. She worked in the library with him. She was the only one there. She claims it was Lisa getting rid of her opponent, but that's just too far out. I mean, come on, let's be realistic here. Who would ever kill for an election to the city council? Not likely, right? Plus his wife has, on several occasions, beaten the crap out of him, sending him to the hospital."

"Has she now?"

"Oh, yes. Abuse in a marriage can go both ways, you see."

"Like this?" I leaned over and kissed Morten on the lips. I closed my eyes and enjoyed it. He grabbed me and pulled me closer. I opened my eyes and stroked him gently across the cheek. He was always so nicely shaved.

"I still think there is something off about that woman though. I just can't put my finger on it," I said.

"Lisa? Yeah. I know what you mean. But sometimes people are just strange, you know. Doesn't have to mean they run around killing people."

"I guess she chose to be a politician instead."

"The lesser of two evils..."

Then we both laughed.

A LETTER FROM WILLOW

Dear Reader,

I want to say a huge thank you for choosing to read *Run, Run, as Fast as You Can*. If you enjoyed it and want to keep up to date with all my latest releases, just sign up at the following link. Your email address will never be shared and you can unsubscribe at any time.

www.bookouture.com/willow-rose

I hope you loved *Run, Run, as Fast as You Can* and if you did, I would be very grateful if you could write a review. I'd love to hear what you think, and it makes such a difference helping new readers to discover one of my books for the first time.

As always, I want to thank you for all your support and for reading my books. I love hearing from my readers—you can get in touch through social media or my website, or email me at madamewillowrose@gmail.com.

Take care,

Willow

KEEP IN TOUCH WITH WILLOW

www.willow-rose.net

- facebook.com/willowredrose
- x.com/madamwillowrose
- instagram.com/willowroseauthor
- bookbub.com/authors/willow-rose

PUBLISHING TEAM

Turning a manuscript into a book requires the efforts of many people. The publishing team at Bookouture would like to acknowledge everyone who contributed to this publication.

Commercial
Lauren Morrissette
Hannah Richmond
Imogen Allport

Cover design
The Brewster Project

Data and analysis
Mark Alder
Mohamed Bussuri

Editorial
Jennifer Hunt
Sinead O'Connor

Proofreader
Joni Wilson

Marketing
Alex Crow
Melanie Price
Occy Carr
Cíara Rosney
Martyna Młynarska

Operations and distribution
Marina Valles
Stephanie Straub

Production
Hannah Snetsinger
Mandy Kullar
Jen Shannon

Publicity
Kim Nash
Noelle Holten
Jess Readett
Sarah Hardy

Rights and contracts
Peta Nightingale
Richard King
Saidah Graham

www.ingramcontent.com/pod-product-compliance
Lightning Source LLC
LaVergne TN
LVHW041630060526
838200LV00040B/1522